IN THE SHELL

Isabel Vallis

Contents

Prologue

The little girl suspected a baka hid within her rag doll collection, its segmented legs concealed by folds of fabric. Although she couldn't see the creature, she sensed its presence. The demon was there, watching her, salivating under all those smiling faces.

She was sure of it.

Once again she peered over the lip of her hammock, but the creature withdrew deeper into its hiding place. No, it was only shadows, she told herself - a trick of the candlelight shifting in the night air. Her mind's just playing games, that's all.

She hadn't slept well since her father left two nights ago. Every shadow was a claw. Every smell, a baka's rotting breath. Even the crickets made her nervous, for this evening they'd fallen deathly quiet.

Her stomach growled in the silence, and that gave her an idea. So she flipped out of her hammock and landed cat-like onto the cold slate. Keeping her eyes on the doll pile, she backed out of her bedroom and hurried into the kitchen. A loaf of bread rested on the table there, left over from dinner. If she laid a slice on the common room floor, maybe the baka would eat that instead of her.

She cut off a chunk and squared it neatly onto a clean plate. The baka would probably like butter, she thought. So she slathered on a generous helping and took a bite. Yes, this would keep her safe. She placed the offering in the common room and shuffled back to her bedroom. Wrestling with her hammock, she settled down under the sheet and listened.

Scratching, from outside.

"Who's there?" she called out, peering back towards the bread and the front door beyond. No one answered. In fact, there were no sounds at all. Usually the desert winds blew spirals of dust under the doorframe. But something now blocked the sand; something crouched on the front step.

"Father, visitors." She hoped the tremble in her voice didn't betray this lie, because right now she was very much alone. Her father wouldn't return from his expedition for several days, maybe a week. But she'd locked the house just like he'd asked, double-checking the bolt to be sure.

She ducked back under the sheet and wrapped it tightly around her head. The cloth barely muffled the noises, however, and a sound more terrifying than the scratching reached her ears: the sharp metal snap of a lock turning.

The baka has a key.

That was impossible. Baka couldn't open locks. The door creaked open, nonetheless, and she heard something scurry into the house.

The little girl didn't want to look, afraid of what she might see. But curiosity finally overcame her fear, and she mustered up enough courage for one final peek.

Everything was silent and still. However, the front door now lay ajar, and a square of moonlight washed over the offering she'd left behind. The little girl stifled a gasp.

Her plate held nothing but crumbs.

Chapter 1

Carlos Consuelo drove east through the tropical heat, marveling at the distance he'd accumulated on his van's odometer. It's not like he had a long commute.

The island of Cayman Brac was tiny, a mere brail dot on the stretch of ocean beneath Cuba. His destination lay nestled along its rocky coast in a bay sheltered from the offshore trade winds. The tin-roofed grocery known as Lalin's Market had become a familiar sight for Carlos. He rumbled into its lot and parked beneath the Poinciana trees at the edge of the Caribbean.

Knocking free the salt crust, he rolled back the van's cargo door and examined the stacks of boxes inside. The morning barge had been packed to the gills, and now so was his Chevy. Where the hell does Mambo expect me to stow all this crap? He ran a calloused hand through the sweat of his hair. Grey flecks showed through the strands now. He was approaching forty, too old for this kind of work.

"Lift with your legs, child," said a diminutive woman with an untraceable accent. She wore a sarong three sizes too large, but the extra cloth didn't slow her down. Mambo Lalin had owned and run the grocery for as long as anyone could remember. The wrinkles in her face gave testament to this. They accentuated her expression, making her smiles wider or - as the case was now - her frowns deeper. She stood in the grocery's doorway, beckoning Carlos to enter. "Hurry, before the rush."

The rush? Carlos had counted a maximum of five people in the store at any one time. And he'd been island bound for six months.

Has it really been that long? Carlos paused for a second and gave it some thought. February he'd taken Henry's advice and left Miami. Took the temp job with the police in April. Now the heat of July was cooking his skin. Six months. He'd been here on the Brac for six months, much longer than he'd anticipated. Over time, however, he'd grown accustomed to island life, which now included sacrificing his off days to help Mambo stock supplies.

He entered the cool of the store, carrying a box of roots. Then he stopped. Lalin's Grocery was so packed with merchandise, he had to let his eyes adjust to the darkness or risk crashing into something.

Several aisles stretched before him, overflowing with cracked jars and boxes sagging with humidity. Gungo Peas, yams, and other foodstuffs jammed every nook, all meticulously labeled in Mambo's illegible scrawl. Dried peppers hung from nets in the rafters. Sugar cane stalks rested against the windows. A chicken pecked the ground beneath the cash register, skirting plastic dollhouses and rows of yard tools. All together, the store's eclectic mix created an earthy smell reminiscent of tortillas, which was odd, as she didn't sell any. He wondered what Mambo would think of the Price Clubs in the states? Woefully under-supplied, he thought. She always has the weirdest crap on stock.

"What the hell is this, Mambo?"

"Mind your tongue." She blinked her eyes at him, a sign she was angry.

"I'm sorry, but I don't think you've got room for all this."

"There'll be plenty of room before long. A storm's brewing." She gestured to the black and white TV suspended above the register. Its grainy image showed a news broadcast from the main island, the swirl of a tropical depression looping endlessly behind the weatherman. Carlos couldn't hear the report, however, as Mambo had her soaps blasting from the radio.

"Think it'll reach us?" he asked. Mambo shuffled up to him and stared directly into his eyes.

"Probably before you unload the van. Galang now." She smiled but her eyes told Carlos something different. The wrinkles tightened involuntarily.

Carlos continued hauling boxes inside, where Mambo directed him towards obscure shelves on which to stock the items. He didn't recognize most of the stuff, but surely chicken feet wouldn't be in high demand for storm survival. Carlos took a break from lifting to chug back a water bottle, when he heard footsteps on the outside gravel.

"Mambo!" came the shrill elderly voice of a woman named Mrs. Sutherland. She wore sunglasses that took up half her face and didn't bother to remove them upon entering. Mambo smiled and hurried to greet her guest.

"I saw something on the north coast road, Mambo. A duppy with red eyes. He was after my little Johnny." The two soon immersed themselves in hushed conversation and headed off towards a far corner of the store. Carlos sighed, familiar with this routine. He knew what Mrs. Sutherland wanted: some kind of protective charm most likely. Mambo served as more than a grocer to many of the older women up in Spot Bay. They still practiced their folk beliefs, much to the consternation of the island clergy. Carlos didn't mind. He'd seen all these religions in Miami - Santeria, Obeah, Vodoun - but wasn't sure which Mambo practiced. Jokingly, he'd once asked her for a voodoo doll. She pinched his ear good for that one. Mambo didn't like to be mocked.

"Carlos, fetch that box for me." Mambo pointed towards a tall shelf. Carlos kicked the footstool into position and reached for the container. It felt surprisingly light, the contents rustling as he lifted it.

"Crabs?" The inside overflowed with several dozen dried crustaceans, their shells stained a dark crimson. Carlos leaned closer. Amongst the eyestalks and claws, he noticed intricate designs painted across each crab's back.

"Cutting costs on charms?"

"Shush. Keep still." Mambo's hand hovered over the box as if performing a magic trick. Finally she selected a medium-sized shell with three purple lines running across its carapace. "This is the one for you. Take it." She smiled and handed it over to Mrs. Sutherland, who cradled it like a rare gem.

"Looks a bit dry," Carlos said. Mambo cast him a look.

"So do you. Shush your mouth." Mambo turned back to her guest. "Take these ingredients and mix them in the shell with castor oil. Light this lamp for seven days and then toss it in the sea." Her wrinkles shifted as she remembered something else. Reaching into her pocketbook, Mambo removed a folded triangle of cloth. "You're going to visit Father McKraggen, yes? Take this to him." She handed the fabric to Mrs. Sutherland and then went to ring up her purchases. Carlos stumbled past, carrying a heavy crate bound to wreck havoc on his back.

* * *

Several miles down the road from Lalin's Market, a cluster of buildings comprised the island's government center. The centerpiece of this quiet village was the Brac museum, a cabin that housed antiquities from the island's past. Its curator - a lanky, bearded man in pressed khaki's - sat at the front desk. Father Henry McKraggen only worked here part time, however. He was first and foremost the island's sole Catholic priest, a title he'd inherited five years ago, when he first marooned himself on the island.

Henry had given up a thriving parish in Miami to come here but never regretted it. The pace of island life allowed time to think, to reflect, to sort things out. That was the reason he'd invited Carlos to join him here. His friend needed a breather. And now it looked like he'd never leave. The island has seduced another victim, Henry thought.

He pushed his spectacles back up the bridge of his nose and returned to the sermon he'd been drafting. It was going badly, and he had a feeling he'd be winging most of it tomorrow. Henry hated winging it.

He twisted his seminary ring around the finger, a habit he repeated whenever lost in thought. Instead of a capstone, the ring's center held a book with the words, "Mysterium Fidei" carved into its pages. The Mystery of Faith.

Henry loved a good mystery, and faith provided more than a fair share. He explored these riddles through sermons - each speech meticulously crafted from bible quotes and personal anecdotes. These fragments became his puzzle pieces, assembled without seeing the picture on the box.

This was his true joy in life: finding the hidden story, researching the unknown, using the light of God to uncover hidden truths. That's a good line, he thought and wrote it down. He scratched his salt and pepper beard for a moment and then erased the entry. It was a terrible line – something out of a greeting card. Crap. Crap. Crap.

He snapped shut his moleskin notebook and secured the bind, then turned his attention to a folder brimming with newspaper clippings. Henry's curiosity extended far beyond sacred matters. He was currently drafting a history of the island, an ambitious undertaking. In fact, he was expecting a visitor today who could help him with this side project.

The front door chimed.

"Hello Ms. Sutherland." Henry smiled at the tiny woman with huge sunglasses.

"I saw a duppy," she told him, "out on the bluff."

Henry gestured to a bench in the museum's gallery, an adjoining room cluttered with fading photos and catboat replicas. "A duppy?" he asked.

"A demon," she said, taking a seat. Henry sighed.

"It was probably a Booby hatchling," he said, referencing the birds of the island.

"I know what I saw." She crossed her arms.

"Ok." Henry didn't want to argue. He had too many questions about the island's history. That was the reason he'd invited Mrs. Sutherland here, after all. She had dubbed herself the oldest living native on the island, and no one disputed the claim. If anyone had the answers for his book it was she.

Henry's manuscript still had two big holes. The first concerned the native Indians on the Brac - specifically, the fact there weren't any. Unlike other islands in the Caribbean, no proof existed that the Taino Indians had ever lived here. No ruins, arrowheads, nothing. Granted the Brac held no fresh water either, but other islands without ground water had been populated. Why not this one?

He didn't think Mrs. Sutherland would know the answer to this. But there was a second disappearance he hoped she could shed some light on. It concerned the English settlers who first called the island home.

"My chapter on the island prior to Emancipation," he began. "I've read accounts of English settlements. But for the life of me, I can't find anyone with descendants that go back that far. I think Spanish pirates might have sacked the island, wiped out everyone. Do you know anybody who has relatives going back that far?"

Mrs. Sutherland shook her head. "My family arrived in 1833 with the Fosters, Waltons, Scotts, and Kirkconnells." She digressed into a lecture on the founding families, which included genealogies so long Henry had to focus to keep himself from nodding off. He'd read sailors' logs describing people on the island prior to the 19th century but nothing to collaborate them. The inhabitants seemed to have vanished, just like the Taino Indians before them. Two mass disappearances, with no explanation for either.

"You should speak with Mambo," Mrs. Sutherland said.

"I thought Mambo's from Cuba."

"That's where she was raised..." Mrs. Sutherland fell uncharacteristically silent. She was about to add something, then caught herself. Instead she said, "Oh, that reminds me," and reached into her purse to remove the cloth Mambo had given her. "This is for our display." The fabric unfurled to reveal a flag sparkling with thousands of sequins.

Henry let out a sigh. He'd reluctantly agreed to an exhibit on the superstitions of the island by Mambo and her elderly friends. Now they were using it to celebrate their folk beliefs, a development that didn't exactly thrill him.

Their display had already doubled in size over the last few weeks. And its contents were becoming more eclectic: jars sealed with dolls inside, some pop bottles wrapped in colorful ribbon, a handful of Caymanite jewelry, and a painting that depicted a grinning skull in a top hat.

"This is too much," Henry said, inspecting the new addition. "Mambo promised me a small exhibit." He knew it was useless arguing with Mambo. If he didn't hang this flag, she'd hear about it through the old lady grapevine and would raise hell. He had to admit, the design was beautiful – a sandcastle of incredible detail.

There must be thousands of sequins in this, he thought. What a labor of love. If only those ladies put that much effort into the church's bake sale; they could finally finish that stained glass window.

Then he noticed something at the base of the sandcastle near the outer wall. A dozen or so sequins formed the image of a man, but the scale was off. He was too small. That must be one hell of a sandcastle, Henry thought. He realized Mrs. Sutherland was still talking and interrupted.

"Thank you. I've got to prepare my sermon now." He stood and ushered her towards the exit. "See you at the prayer brunch tomorrow?" But Mrs. Sutherland stood on the porch and spoke for another twenty minutes. Definitely winging that sermon, Henry thought. Lord, give me patience.

Chapter 2

Sunday morning debuted with a clear sky. Despite this and optimistic radio bulletins, Mambo was still convinced the storm would strike the island and kept her store open. When the morning past without a single customer, she decided she'd warn her fellow parishioners in person. So she'd called Carlos and convinced him to give her a lift to church.

Carlos grumbled under his breath, his morning fishing plans now ruined. Today was his daughter's birthday, and he'd felt like spending it alone. They rumbled west along the coast in silence, windows rolled down for the breeze.

Finally Carlos asked, "Is this a sales gimmick?" Mambo didn't reply, her eyes closed, head resting against the belt strap. "You're just going to panic folks. The storm's passed."

"Shush, they must be warned," she said without moving. Carlos gave up and turned to watch a frigate bird gliding overhead. It followed the coastal road, buoyed by updrafts from the cliffs nearby. From that height, he knew the island resembled a giant doorstop, ramping skyward towards the bluff at one end. Henry once told him these cliffs gave the Brac its name, a Gaelic word apparently. Well, cliffs were definitely the most prominent feature here on the island's eastern point. Made sense to name the island after them.

The tiny village of Spot Bay lay nestled beneath the bluff, on the narrow coastal plain sandwiched between the rocks and the sea. Carlos waved at the old men in their pressed suits as he idled past. Spot Bay was an old town; most of the youth had moved off the island as soon as they were able. Those who returned seldom left the Brac again. Carlos wondered if he ever would. No, they'll probably bury me in one of those plots overlooking the sea, right next to Henry and Mambo. He began to pass cars parked on either side of the road, a sign they were getting close.

By the time they reached the small, whitewashed church at the end of the bay, the service had already concluded. People were gathered on the lawn just beyond the beach, where tabletops strained under trays of conch fritters, sticky buns, and lemonade pitchers. Nearby, a truck dispensed homemade ice cream to a throng of children with their hands outstretched. Carlos heard their laughter as he parked his van on a side road near the cliffs.

"Lock your door please," he reminded Mambo as they exited. She snorted and left the door unlocked.

Carlos heard a loud bark. Looking over, he saw Salty, a scruffy Labrador and official mascot of Salty's, the Spot Bay tavern. This flea hound often accompanied him on fishing trips to Bamboo Bay. Salty could smell Yellowfin a mile off. If it weren't for Mambo, the two of them would be out there right now.

"Hey there, boy. How's my fishing partner?" But Salty wasn't wagging his tail in welcome. He'd tucked it defensively between his legs. The dog's eyes narrowed and locked on a nearby patch of sea grapes. He started to growl.

"What is it? What do you see?"

Nothing moved in the leaves. The dog barked again sharply and then looked up at Carlos as if urging him on to the church.

"Dogs have a keener sense than you or me." Mambo squinted into the surrounding foliage.

"He's getting jumpy in his old age. You need to relax, Salty." Carlos scratched the dog behind his ears and then followed the scampering mutt across the main road and into the churchyard.

"Don't let Salty in here," came the sardonic voice Carlos knew so well. "He knows we have ribs." Henry stood alone over the barbecue pit, cooking tongs in hand.

"Yeah. He's unhappy you're not sharing..." Carlos slapped hands with his old buddy. "Father McKraggen, sorry I missed the service."

"That's all right," Henry said straight-faced. "You'll just be going to Hell."

"Beats listening to you." Carlos snatched a handful of muffins off the table and began juggling them.

"Good morning, Ms. Lalin," Henry said, noticing Mambo for the first time. "How're things at the store?"

"They are slow, and they shouldn't be."

"Well, it is Sunday."

Mambo blinked her eyes rapidly. She put her hands on her hips. "People need things for the storm." She waved at the other parishioners, and they strolled over to join them. Mambo served as surrogate mother to half the island population, and everyone loved her company.

"Are we in its path?" Henry asked. "Radio Cayman said the islands were clear —"

"No matter what they say, a storm's coming." By the tone in her voice, everyone knew better than to speak against her. A few of the older women even nodded in agreement. Henry smiled graciously and tried to change the subject.

"Well, if you're open, I might come by later and get some wax for my board."

Mambo clucked her tongue disapprovingly. "You shouldn't be out on the water at your age. Surfing 'round like some bobo." She began rooting through her oversized handbag, while Henry smiled nervously. "I have something for you," she continued.

"Mrs. Sutherland already brought by that flag," Henry protested. "There's not room for any —"

"This is not for the museum. For your own protection."

"She must've heard about your sermon," Carlos laughed and stopped juggling. Henry cast him a sideways glance. An awkward silence passed over the group, but Mambo didn't seem to mind. She eventually found what she'd been searching for – a tiny bottle wrapped in ribbons with feathers sprouting from the top. Henry's face flashed annoyance, but he quickly masked it.

"Really, Ms. Lalin. I'm not superstitious. A little prayer does the —"

"Trust me. You're gonna need this for the storm." She pressed the charm into his hands, and Henry quickly pocketed it from view. "I'm going to warn the rest of the folks here." Mambo smiled and pressed on into the crowd, humming a gospel hymn under her breath.

Eager to change the subject, a young woman in a blue flower-dress asked, "Have you written about the storm of '32 in your book?"

"Yes. It's well documented," Henry said. "What I'm having trouble with are some of the early chapters, gaps in the history there. I spoke to Mrs. Sutherland about it. Well, she did most of the speaking." The group laughed, well acquainted with the island matriarch and her gift of gab.

A hopeful gleam came into Henry's eyes. "If the storm does come close, there might be some good rollers."

The grin disappeared from Carlos's face. He was wise to his friend's surfing passion – more of an addiction really. Carlos guessed the ocean provided him with an escape from his needy congregation, a chance to be alone for a few hours. It was the same reason Henry enjoyed scuba diving and rock climbing so much. "You be careful, old man. Ocean's not something to mess with. And you're no spring chicken."

"The Lord'll look after me."

"Isn't that what the devil tempted Christ with? Daring him to cheat death?"

Henry clasped his hands together and smiled. "So you do pay attention. Yes, he dared Christ to jump from a tower and let the angels catch him. Messianic skydiving." He conceded the point. "However, I do take precautions," and gazing out to sea, he added, "The weather doesn't look too stormy out there anyway."

As if to contradict his words, the wind whipped up at that moment, sending paper plates and napkins flying across the church grounds. People scrambled to secure the tablecloth. Instead of helping, Carlos used the distraction to drop a muffin. Salty swallowed it with one bite and looked up expectantly. Before he could grab another treat, however, a young couple approached them. Carlos could sense they wanted to talk to their minister alone. Poor guy, Carlos thought, one man taking on all the sorrows of the island.

"You want to head to Salty's for dinner?" he asked. It was more of a statement than a question really. Salty's was the local hangout, and they ate there practically every night.

"After I swing by Mambo's. Grab some emergency supplies." Henry smiled. "Never hurts to stock up."

"You're a good man," Carlos said, slapping his friend on the back.

* * *

Salty's, the island's unofficial town hall, news station, and watering hole stood at the base of the cliffs, surrounded by tropical foliage. Night had already descended on the bay, and the lights of the tavern beckoned invitingly as Carlos pulled his van into the lot. Judging from the lack of cars, they wouldn't have to wait for a table tonight.

He was right. The place was nearly deserted, just a scattering of locals and a tourist couple in Hawaiian shirts.

"Hey Carlos." The bar keep waved and patted the counter in front of him. Carlos pulled up a stool next to Henry and began nursing a pint of Brac Brew, a sweet coconut drink and island favorite.

Lanterns illuminated the paneling around them, which resembled the woodwork of a boat's hull. Henry had once explained the tavern's origins to Carlos - how an old shrimper had washed ashore and been converted into a restaurant. Despite the overhaul, the structure still retained its portholes, curved walls, and other nautical features. A tarnished mirror above the bar doubled the size of the room and gave the guys a view of the interior.

"Where is everyone tonight?" Carlos asked.

"You hear about the hurricane?" the bar tender asked.

"Hurricane?"

"Yup. Just upgraded it. Stalled apparently. Will likely reverse course - come straight at us. I'm closing early tonight. Got to start boarding the windows."

Carlos groaned. Mambo's premonition had come true. He'd never hear the end of it.

"Can you bring some food to the shelter?" he asked the bar keep. "I think they're low on supplies." The government had just assembled a reinforced building on the interior of the island. It had cost a fortune but had yet to be tested.

"Sure thing. I'll just add it to your tab."

Carlos smiled. "Thanks."

"I don't know if I'd trust that tin can," Henry said. "Back before it was built people used the caves for shelter."

"Yeah, nothing says cozy like a dark, muddy cave." Carlos slung back a gulp of beer.

"Whatchya talk'n about?" They looked over to see a small woman ambling up to them.

"Oh no, Mrs. Sutherland." Henry hid behind his beer flask, but it was too late. She'd already pulled up a stool next to his.

"You know people got pulled right out of those caves," she said, "back when the storm of '32 hit."

Henry put on his best smile and turned back around. "Mrs. Sutherland, why're you wearing sunglasses? It's dark out."

"I meant to tell you about Mrs. Bodden's grandchild, Rebecca. You've got to mention her in your book."

"Well, if there's room. It's not an encyclopedia."

Mrs. Sutherland opened her mouth to respond, but a murderous howl interrupted her. The entire tavern froze. They heard another yelp and then a terrible hiss.

"Salty?" the bar tender yelled. Everyone rushed to get outside. Carlos led the group into the parking lot, his training taking over. In the low light he could barely make out some movement, a dark form rustling in one of the empty parking spaces.

"Hit the floods," he whispered. Soon the lot filled with blinding spotlights. It took Carlos a moment to process the horrible image before him; he'd never seen anything like it and hoped he never would again. In the sand between two Jeeps lay Salty, a pool of blood collecting at his side. Gash wounds exposed a bit of the dog's ribcage. His tongue rolled out of a lifeless snout. Clearly, he was dead. But his carcass still moved as something chewed at it. A pale creature, about the size of a pig, crouched low behind the body. When hit by the light, it raised two huge claws in defense, then turned and scuttled sideways into the foliage.

"It's a crab," Carlos heard himself say. But he'd never heard of a crab that size let alone one that could move so fast. A stunned silence washed over the tavern's patrons.

A crab killed him? What the hell kind of crab could do that? It was like something out of the night terrors he used to get as a kid.

Henry rushed to the dog's side and knelt down. No pulse. He shook his head: Salty was gone. Shouts of anger rose from the other regulars. Carlos balled a fist and then bounded past them, straight into the dark jungle.

A dozen creatures scurried away as he entered the woods, but none sounded as large as the crab. With one quick movement, Carlos reached to his side and unsheathed a buck knife he kept strapped there. He could hear a few of the bar regulars following close behind him. Soon flashlight beams criss-crossed the palmetto underbrush. Carlos held up his hand. He wanted nothing more than swift revenge but wouldn't sacrifice anyone's safety for it.

"If we keep after it, we'll just flush it into town...and that's the last thing we want." The others nodded their agreement. The cliff rose a few feet to their right. Following its base would lead them to the first houses of Spot Bay. "We've got to warn them." Carlos realized that he'd taken command of the situation. It was the first time he'd done anything like that since Miami. "We'll drive," he said.

The first homes weren't far away, but Carlos pressed the gas pedal to the floor. His van spun out onto the coastal road and then turned down the next side street. Only three homes bordered the woods, but he knew that each of them had kids. Parking the van, he was about to knock on the first door, when he heard children's screams. They came from the backyard.

Carlos vaulted over a chicken wire fence and sprinted across the Astroturf. Rounding the house, he saw a group of children running. They were chasing fireflies, screaming with glee whenever they caught one.

"Listen up," Carlos called out. "I need everyone to go inside." When a few protested he raised his voice. "Get the hell outta here." Their eyes widened. "Now," he screamed.

The children bolted for the screened porch. Carlos took out his knife and approached the wood line. His whole chest heaved with exhaustion. Or maybe it was adrenaline. The crab hid nearby; he could sense it.

Behind him, Henry staggered into the yard. "You ok?"

"Are the children inside?" Carlos asked, his heart racing.

"Yeah, they're safe. I'll tell their parents about Salty."

Carlos thought of his canine fishing partner, panting happily across the rowboat. He grimaced. Poor Salty. He flashed his Maglite into the dense foliage, but the beam revealed only mango trees and cacti. No sign of the crab. So he sheathed his knife, almost splitting its holder in the process.

Henry put a hand on his friend's shoulder to calm him. "He died quickly."

"I'm going to find that damn thing."

"Shouldn't be too hard. You see that paint on its back? Ever seen anything like that?"

"Yeah, actually I have," Carlos said. He'd seen something like that earlier in the day - on Mambo's crab charms. The exact same designs adorned those shells. Something in his gut told him this was no coincidence.

Chapter 3

The black & white above the register flashed grainy images of the approaching hurricane. The storm had reversed course during the night and even picked up speed. As a result, the morning rush had already cleared out the grocery's bottled water and half its canned goods. Carlos purchased some Advil and immediately popped two pills. He had bags under his eyes from searching the woods all-night, late into dawn. But they'd found no trace of the crab, not even a blood trail. So he'd spent the rest of the morning warning folks about the approaching storm. Now he'd returned to Mambo's grocery to help her board up the place.

Towards lunch, the customers dwindled, returning home to secure their houses before the hurricane made landfall. Carlos wanted to wait until they were completely alone before asking her about the crab, but Mambo seemed to anticipate his question; word of the creature had spread quickly across the island. They were halfway through boarding up the windows when she broached the subject.

"Just ask me, child."

"What?"

"Something's bugging you." She placed a wrinkled hand on his to prevent him from nailing another board. "Ask your question."

"You know that thing you gave Ms. Sutherland yesterday?"

"The charm?"

"Yeah, the shell covered in lines. Well, yesterday, the crab that killed Salty —"

"Had the same marks on him?"

"In blood. It looked like it had painted itself."

"Yes, a terrible thing."

"You know about this type of crab?"

Mambo Lalin took a deep breath. "Yes, I know about this." She waved goodbye to the last customer and then went inside the store. Shuffling over to the register, she grabbed her key ring from the counter.

"Well, what species is that? Salty was old...but I never heard of a crab that could —"

"This is no crab," Mambo said, thumbing through her collection of keys. She had so many, the ring resembled a sea urchin.

"Sure looked like a crab to me."

Mambo found what she was looking for - an ornate key much older than the others.

"Are they native to the island?"

"No, not the Brac." She put a gnarled finger to her lips and beckoned Carlos to follow. Then she turned and walked towards the back of the shop. "You're going to need some things."

"I don't need charms, Mambo. I told you, I'm Catholic."

"So am I," she said.

A tiny wharf stretched out from the back of the store; it was more a loose collection of planks, lined with poles, buoys, and other flotsam and jetsam. The path ended abruptly at a shack suspended above the tide pools. Carlos had always wondered what she kept in this structure and had eventually decided upon overflow storage.

"You've never seen my peristyle, have you?" She placed the key into the lock.

Carlos smiled. "I was saving that for our wedding night."

She shot him an irritated look and opened the door. It took Carlos a moment to register what he was seeing. Flags lined the interior of the shed, hundreds of them. Their fabric had long ago faded, but the embroidery caught Carlos's eye. Incredible detail had been woven into the silk: images of skulls, hearts, and waterfalls. Carlos recognized them as ceremonial voodoo flags called drapos, highly prized by the Miami art crowd. His ex-wife owned quite a few.

"You collect Haitian art, Mambo?"

"These aren't Haitian," she said.

Looking closer, he saw that she was right. Most of the drapos depicted very strange imagery. One showed warriors in flowing gowns stabbing their spears at enormous crabs, another a tower looming high above the ocean. Carlos was so taken by the flags, he rammed his shin into a circular table in the middle of the room. It was completely bare save for a wooden pole, which rose from its surface up into the rafters. Mambo motioned for him to take a seat.

He rubbed the bruise and tried not to curse. "Where did you get these flags then? Cuba?"

"You want to know about the baka?" Mambo asked.

"Yes, if that's what you call these crabs." He sat on one of the woven chairs scattered about the room.

"Not crabs." Mambo sighed and cracked her knuckles. "A baka is a devil, a dangerous one."

"Where do these...baka come from? The ocean?"

"Greedy, evil men bring them...they make a deal with the baka. And for that, they get money and power."

Carlos shifted uncomfortably. He had hoped Mambo would know where on the island these crabs lived. Instead, it looked like he'd get a lecture on voodoo theology. He'd have to steer the conversation back on topic.

"Do the baka live on the bluff or down by the coast?"

"The Baka don't live on the Brac. If one is here, it means there's great trouble on the island." Mambo hesitated as if the words were painful to speak. "As the evil men grow more powerful, so do the baka. And they demand payment...horrible payment."

"The baka demand payment?" Carlos asked, deciding to humor her. It was clear he couldn't control this interview. On patrol in Miami he'd learned it was often best to play along and let the informant tell you in their own way.

"Yes, the baka demand the souls of the innocent."

"These baka will attack people?"

Mambo nodded sadly. "Without mercy."

"When was the last time you saw one?"

"Years ago."

She didn't elaborate so Carlos pressed on. "Ok, so how do we find these baka and kill them?"

"First, you must find the evil men who've dealt with the demons. They will lead you to the baka."

Carlos rolled his eyes. "Let's focus on the creatures first. Do they all draw designs on their backs?"

"They mark their kills," Mambo said. "You've stopped evil men in Miami?"

"Yeah, a few of them." He didn't feel like reminiscing.

She locked eyes with him. "Then you're up to the task. I heard how you saved the children last night."

Carlos ran a hand through his hair. This was going nowhere. Mambo thought sorcery controlled the crabs, so naturally her solution was to go after the sorcerer. "Ok, I find these evil men, stop them from helping the creatures, and that'll lead me to the baka."

"Yes." She smiled, pleased that he understood.

"After the storm passes, I'll look into it." He stood up to go. "We should really finish with the windows."

Mambo's face tightened. "This is no joke. " She yanked him back down with surprising strength. "You'll need some things."

Carlos smiled. "I think my buck knife is enough for any crab."

To Carlos's surprise, Mambo unsheathed a curved sword from behind the door. "Even this may not save you from the baka."

"Whoa, Mambo...be careful."

Mambo sheathed the sword and set the scabbard in front of Carlos. "Take it. You can fend off the smaller ones."

Carlos bent forward to inspect the carvings on the scabbard, images of crabs with twisted claws and cat-like eyes. Someone had quite an imagination. As he studied the designs, a wind kicked up and rattled the boards of the hut, sending the silk drapos into a fury.

"We should get back to securing the store —"

"That can wait." Mambo was stern. "This cannot."

She opened a golden box, stuffed with an expensive velvet cushion. Nestled in its folds, like an oyster's pearl, lay a single glass marble, which Mambo brought into the light. The orb swirled dark with a viscous liquid. "Be careful," she said, handing it over. "This can kill forty men."

"Forty men? What is it, cyanide?"

"No, it comes from a fish in the sea. Very deadly. Very dangerous. For the larger baka."

"Mambo, we don't have time for these charms."

"Charms! Is that what you think these are?" She threw her hands to her hips. "You have no idea what you're in for, boy. So shush your face."

"Ok, fine." She'd never used that tone before with him. This was obviously very important to her. No more jokes.

"And last, you must take this." She bent down and removed one of her many necklaces and placed it on the table. It held a round medallion at one end, the design a strange shape he didn't recognize.

"This looks expensive. I can't take all this," Carlos said.

"You must, or you will die," Mambo said with such conviction it startled him. "Now, we have precious little time before the storm arrives."

"Wait a minute. You still haven't told me —"

But Mambo had already cast open the door. Wind drowned out his words and buffeted the sari wildly about her hips, revealing the contours of an insulin pump she wore there. When she finally turned around, Carlos caught his breath. A look of intense fear had drained the life from her face. He'd never seen Mambo use this expression and didn't care to see it again; her sunken eyes stared back fiercely.

"A baka like this, like a crab, he comes from the island beneath the sea." Her face softened. "You must find the way on your own, child. It won't be easy. But I trust you can make it."

Chapter 4

The following day, the island braced itself for the coming storm. Mambo sold or gave away all her emergency supplies, and Carlos spent the day ferrying people to the airport. Many folks had chosen to flee the Brac for the safety of Grand Cayman.

Those that remained found their way to the shelter. Volunteers had already assembled rows of cots here, with the best spots going fast. Carlos paced the concrete floor near the restrooms.

"Damn it," he muttered to himself. "He's gonna be stuck next to Mrs. Sutherland all night." He clicked on his CB radio, listening through the bursts of static, as he checked over the contents of his pack.

"Hurricane Daphne has been upgraded to a category 4 storm," crackled the latest bulletin. "Residents of the sister islands should seek immediate shelter."

"Where the hell is he?" Carlos weaved through the sea of people, until he got to the door and peered out. The sky had turned dark, rain streaked by, and wind rattled the nearby palms. Pretty soon the brunt of the storm would reach them.

"Hold the door." One of the elders from Spot Bay came running across the grass, clutching his hat.

"Have you see Henry?" Carlos yelled.

"Yes, damn fool's out on the ocean."

"Oh no, he's not."

"Gonna get himself killed."

"Damn it. Was it Spot Bay?"

"Yes, out past the point. Tried to call him in, but he couldn't hear me."

Grabbing the rain slicker from his backpack, Carlos zippered tight and shouldered out into the storm. He jumped into his police cruiser, an old Crown Victoria, and peeled out for the coast. Every passing second, the storm grew worse, decreasing his chances of finding Henry alive.

In his rear view mirror, Carlos glimpsed the receding form of Mambo staring at him from the shelter's doorway. Then rain obscured her image entirely. The hurricane was upon them.

* * *

Henry had never seen waves like this - each one a beauty, strong and sculpted with motion. With the sky darkening beyond, it made him feel utterly alone with the elements. He paddled ahead of a huge swell and mounted his board. The coastline reeled up ahead of him, and he realized that he was now looking down on the rooftops of Spot Bay. The wave was much larger than he'd thought – its roar thundering as the curl started to collapse. Henry pressed hard into the curve and managed to stay ahead of the break. The water rushed below him at highway speeds. To wipeout here would be deadly. He leaned forward, but realized he was losing ground. The curl of the wave enveloped him, and before he knew it, he was spinning in an avalanche of foam. His lungs cried out in pain. Which way is up? Black dots started to form in his eyes.

Carlos reached out and grabbed Henry under the arm. Then he kicked towards the surface, where they both gasped at the sweet oxygen.

"Did you see that ride?" Henry cried hoarsely. Carlos didn't bother responding. He continued to drag Henry towards shore until they could both stand. However, the next few waves brought them both to their knees and spit them out on the pebble beach like driftwood.

"What the hell do you think you're doing?" Carlos yelled over the howling wind.

"I couldn't pass that up."

"You almost died, you idiot."

"Where's my board?" Henry asked.

"You want to go back and get it?" Carlos pointed at the ocean, which churned angrily like a washing machine on spin.

"Yes, it won't take long —"

"Forget the damn board." Carlos pulled him towards the car. "We've got to get to shelter."

Henry dug his heels into the pebbles. "I've a lot of fond memories of that board." When he turned back around, his jaw dropped; pieces of his surfboard bobbed in the foam like crackers on a soup. The rocks had torn the polystyrene to shreds.

"That could have been you," Carlos said. "Let's go."

The two men scrambled across the pebbles towards the parking lot. A sudden gust overhead sent the palmettos whipping about like cheerleader pom-poms and blasted them with debris. Waterlogged, they piled into the Victoria, where Carlos pulled on his boots and wasted no time flooring the gas pedal. Even on full, the windshield wipers barely kept the road ahead visible.

"Has everyone left Spot Bay?" Henry asked, after a period of roaring silence.

"It's a Category 4, what do you think?"

"I should've left earlier."

"Really?"

Plywood coated every home they past, the streets now resembling a ghost town. Above the roofs, clouds spun slowly in claustrophobic spirals. Lightning lit up their inner bands, then plunged the road into darkness as black as coal.

"Watch out," Henry yelled.

A Sabal Palm splashed down directly in front of them, barricading the road out of town. Carlos swerved to a stop, and the two men got out to inspect the obstacle. It had taken down a power line, which sparked amongst the fronds like an electric eel.

"It's too heavy," Carlos said, cursing under the weight of the trunk. "We'll have to —"

A horrible metal screech interrupted him. Beyond the roadblock, the two men witnessed a corrugated roof peel off from its house like a tin can lid and slice into a nearby mahogany grove.

"Caves!" Henry yelled over the wind. Carlos nodded his agreement and threw himself back into the driver's seat. They drove down the side road to the base of the cliffs and parked at the trailhead there. The path ahead switch-backed up the rocks to a gaping hole in the wall that commanded a wide view of the bay. This would provide the best shelter – if they could make it. Carlos grabbed his knapsack from the back seat. Swinging it over his shoulder, he started up the steep trail. Before they'd made much progress, however, the two men heard trees snapping and glanced down in time to see the Victoria's roof crumple under a mass of wet branches. There was no going back now. The wind blasted at them full force. Carlos could feel it prying his fingers from the rock.

"Go," he yelled, but his words were drowned out in the gale force blast. Henry dug in and made it to the opening – surprising since his booties didn't provide much traction. He reached back to give Carlos a hand and just in time. At that moment, the full brunt of the hurricane fell upon them; rain and dirt pelted their sides like buckshot. The wind took hold of Carlos and lifted him feet-first from the rock. But Henry straddled two stalagmites, and pulled with all his strength - only his grip now preventing Carlos from tumbling away into the storm.

From his friend's expression, Carlos could tell the Gates of Hell had opened up behind him. He felt one of his boots slide off; the

Timberland sucked into a vortex of rain and wind. With all his might, he willed his free hand up and grabbed a hold of Henry's wrist. Then the wind died - and as if propelled from a cannon - the men flew backwards into the mouth of the cave. They tumbled down a muddy incline, slid past stalagmites, and came to a messy stop beneath a fragile calcite drapery.

"Damn your surfing," Carlos said and punched Henry in the arm. The two gasped for breath, high on survival adrenaline. Carlos had experienced close scrapes before, but they'd been in the line of duty. Now that he was pushing forty, his body couldn't take the beating anymore. He shook his head, angry with himself for actually enjoying all this.

"I'll pay for the car damage, Carl. I'm sorry." Henry massaged a bruise he'd received on the way in. Then he tilted his head and tried to get the water out of his ear.

Carlos wanted to punch him again. "You're sorry? Jesus, Henry. What the hell were you thinking?"

"I wasn't," Henry admitted, patting his head until the water leaked out. Then he sighed. "But I did feel the hand of God out there."

"Yeah, he smacked you upside the head with it. Hopefully knocked some sense into you." Gradually, the adrenaline wore off. Carlos paused, cocking his ear to the side. "You hear that?"

"I don't hear anything."

"Exactly."

They scrambled back to the rim of the cave and peered out. The wind had tapered off now, and rain slowed to a drizzle. Cool air flooded down from above.

"The eye," Henry said in a whisper. Carlos felt it too, as if speaking any louder would disturb the tenuous balance and bring back the storm. An awesome sight lay before them - the remains of Spot bay strewn about with palm shreds and other debris. A tsunami-sized cloudbank curved overhead, which Carlos realized was the inner edge of the hurricane twisting just offshore. Bands of thunderheads moved along its perimeter, illuminated every now and then from lightning deep within its folds. Carlos clenched his teeth as the thunder reverberated through his jawbone.

"It's going to get bad again. Here take this." He removed a flashlight from his backpack and tossed it to Henry.

"You came prepared."

"I've known you long enough." Carlos cinched tight a headlamp for himself and proceeded towards the rear of the cave. "How deep does this thing go?"

"Not sure." Henry glanced back at the entrance. "I bet it's extensive."

"Well, we can't stay here," Carlos said. A chilled wind ruffled his jacket. "Come on. The eye's passing."

The two ducked their way through a slick maze of flowstone until they could no longer see daylight. A grotto opened up ahead with a bowl providing enough room to stand. Instead, they collapsed onto the ground. Carlos lit a tea candle, which cast its meager light onto the helictite formations nearby. After his eyes had adjusted, he rummaged through his pack and exchanged the wet clothes for dry ones he'd brought with him. He threw Henry a spare sweater.

"You have any food in there?" Henry asked.

"Not for you, Evel Knievel."

"Look, I apologized already. We're safe now."

"I was safer in Miami." Carlos tossed a Granola bar to his friend. "I don't need this drama."

"Then why don't you move back?" Henry peeled off the wrapper and took a bite. "I never thought you'd settle here."

You and me both, thought Carlos. When he'd first accepted Henry's invitation, he'd only planned on staying a few weeks, not months. He still couldn't believe how time had flown.

"Not that I want to get rid of you." Henry smiled gently. "I'll probably live longer with you around. So take all the time you need to sort things out..."

Carlos shot his friend an annoyed look. "This ain't a confessional."

"No, but we've never really talked —"

"Ok, Padre. Enough." Carlos gathered a handful of rocks from the ground and passed three to Henry. Then he bent his arms to his chest in the standard juggling position. Henry mirrored his actions, and they did a few passes before one of the stones went awry.

"Violet was better at this than you," Carlos said, handing him back the rock.

"I need more practice before we try passing. Juggling's not —"

"Son of a bitch," Carlos interrupted, dropping his rocks.

"Whoa, take it easy."

"Don't move." He unfastened his buck knife.

"What is it?" Henry asked, frozen in place. Carlos mouthed back the word 'crab', his eyes locked on the ledge above Henry's head.

"You're kidding."

The creature eyed him from across the room, candlelight flickering in its eye stocks. It was definitely the same one he'd seen the other night– Salty's dried blood was still splattered across its shell. The crab carefully placed one leg backward. Carlos gripped his knife tighter. Then without warning he swung forward and released the blade. It whizzed thru the air and ricocheted off the surprisingly hard shell. The crab hissed furiously and toppled, leg's scrambling, onto Henry's shoulders.

"Mother," Henry screamed and threw it off. The crab regained its balance and opened its claws in attack position. They snapped erratically, like a lethal pair of hedge clippers. "What the hell kind of crab is that?"

"One that's hard to kill," Carlos said, "but its going to pay for what it did to Salty. Take the knife and chase it towards me." Henry hesitated, then picked up the weapon and charged after the crab, which scurried away into the darkness.

Carlos knelt and unzipped his pack. He removed the sword that Mambo had given him, drawing it from the scabbard. A shrill ring echoed immediately throughout the cavern. In the glow of his headlamp's LED, the metal gleamed back an unworldly blue. It seemed sharp enough, however. He tried a few practice swings and was surprised how natural it felt in his hands. Soon he heard Henry's voice.

"I think I got the bastard cornered."

"Where are you?" He saw a flicker of light ahead and aimed for it.

"It's coming your way." His beam caught the scurrying form of the crab racing across the mud. It immediately ducked left to avoid his light and crouched behind the stub of a stalagmite. Carlos pounced, the sword arcing over his head. But the crab saw him coming and skittered out of the way just as the blade sliced down.

"Fast little sucker, isn't he?" Henry said, panting for breath. Then he saw the sword. "Where'd you get that?"

"Mambo."

Carlos wiped the blade free of dirt, ducked under an arch, and hurried down a ramp onto a flat, sandy floor. His head bumped a few soda straws on the ceiling, so he bent low as he scanned the chamber. There was no telling how wide the room extended because his light faded to black in all directions. But he did see tracks leading away, and that was all he needed. With Henry close in tow, he jogged forward into a labyrinth of columns, many stained red from trace oxides in the stone. The tracks grew fainter here, and Carlos realized that the ground was becoming harder. Soon he'd lost the trail completely.

"Damn."

"He can't be far. I just heard scrambling," Henry said. They both stopped in place and listened. But it was no use. Outside of Henry's labored breathing, it was deathly quiet. Even the hurricane's wind didn't penetrate this far into the cave.

"Watch out!" Henry shouted and pointed. Carlos instinctively swung wide with his sword. The creature had been lodged directly above them on the ceiling. It released its grip and fell at Carlos's neck. Before it reached him, however, the crab and blade connected with a sickening crunch. The carapace shattered. Blood sprayed across the sand. The creature fell to the ground, hissing and squealing. Finally, it lay still. The crab was dead. Carlos wiped the sweat from his brow and bent down to inspect his kill.

"Looks exotic," he said. "Definitely not native." That was an understatement. The creature resembled a horror movie prop, legs twisting backward in a hideous death curl. Easily the largest crab he'd ever seen, there were other details that gave Carlos pause. The legs appeared longer and thicker for one thing, and the shell harder, almost like the metal plating from his old SWAT vest. But what struck him the most were the creature's eyes. Large and alien, almost cat-like – they stared lifelessly back at him.

"Give me the buck knife."

Henry handed it over, then asked, "What are you doing?"

"Getting a souvenir." Carlos sawed at one of the claws. "Look at this thing. The detail in the designs." He focused his headlamp at the carcass. Bloodstains caught the light – a precise series of spirals on the creature's shell, too artistic to be natural.

"Someone painted him," Henry said. Carlos nodded in agreement. The buck knife crunched as it severed a joint.

"Check this out." Carlos held up the claw and pointed to the unmistakable white knob of a humerus bone.

"Crabs don't have skeletons," Henry said, "...on this inside anyway."

"Yeah, just shells...but this one has bones." Carlos began ripping apart the body. "A complete set, skull and everything. Check out the size of its brain."

"Yeah, I'd rather not." Henry turned away.

Carlos had been to enough crab bakes to know the inside of a crustacean pretty well. And this creature was totally different. Once dissected, it more closely resembled the autopsy photos from his old case files. The brains alone were the size of a dried apple. That sent a queasy sensation to the pit of his stomach. It wasn't nausea, more like apprehension.

"Why did you bring the sword?" Henry asked.

"Mambo was determined I take it. " Carlos returned the weapon to his pack.

"Hmmm." Henry scratched his beard. "All she gives me are those feather dusters."

"And I'm sure you keep every one." Carlos was about to recount his full conversation with Mambo, then thought better of it. Henry barely tolerated Mambo's folk traditions, so it was doubtful he'd warm to her theory on the crab's origins. What had she called them, baka?

"You remember how we got back here?" Henry asked. This gave Carlos pause. Which direction did we come from? Left? Right? He'd been so caught up in killing the crab, he'd lost track.

"Shit," he said. "Well, let's pick a direction. We're bound to see our footprints." They headed out, but the harder soil beneath their feet extended for quite a ways, and there was no sign they'd even tread this way. However, something else certainly had.

What Carlos saw next, took his breath away. As the sand ahead became softer, he noticed dozen of tracks criss-crossing the surface – all of them crab.

"He was all over this section," Henry said.

"I hope it was just him. Look, there's the ramp we came down."

"Are you sure that's the same one? I don't see our footprints."

"Well, the crab came down it. So there's got to be a way out." Carlos sighed, tucked the claw into his belt, and began scrambling up the steep incline. "We're gonna lose batteries soon."

"How many candles do you have?" Henry asked.

"Just one more." He lit a match and held it to the wick. Once the flame caught, the two men switched off their flashlights and trudged on in silence.

Chapter 5

Hours later and the candle had melted down to a stub. Carlos now realized they faced dozens of identical ramps, all inter-connected like a house of mirrors. The multi-tiered columns looked familiar and yet frustratingly new at each turn, providing no references whatsoever.

The whole bluff must be honeycombed with caves, Carlos thought. He'd always guessed such a labyrinth lay beneath the ground. On the surface, he'd often marveled at the cracks and holes pocketing the sharp, rocky landscape. Devil's Meringue is what the locals called this topography. Now that they were trapped inside this demonic desert, with no bearings or water, the name seemed especially apt.

They were about to settle down for the night, when Carlos spotted a slit in the wall, a trail of crab tracks leading out from it. Turning sideways, he eased through the crack into the open space beyond.

"Henry, come here...quick." The two men found themselves atop a chasm so deep, the candlelight couldn't illuminate its bottom. But the rift wasn't what held their attention; an ancient bridge spanned the blackness. It led to another opening in the flowstone, a hundred yards away.

"Think its safe?" Henry asked, peering into the void.

Carlos stared at his friend incredulously. "You're not thinking of crossing that?" A tangle of grass rope was all that supported the bridge. Someone had threaded boards through the fibers to create a primitive walkway.

Henry stamped the wood to test its age. "Why not? Has to lead somewhere."

"But we're looking for the exit."

Ignoring his friend's protests, Henry felt the woven railings. "This could be the work of the Taino." He began to rotate his seminary ring, a gleam flashing in his eyes. They might've stumbled upon a rare archeological find, proof native peoples had once lived on the Brac. Perhaps they left artifacts, pots or statuary.

Henry licked his lips.

"Let's test it first." Carlos picked up a stone and tossed it into the abyss. They waited in silence for several seconds before a splash came echoing back. "Water. That's a long way down." He looked up and saw that Henry was already halfway across the bridge. "Jesus..."

Carlos followed his friend over the planks and through the crack on the opposite side. They entered into what appeared to be a construction tunnel - no stalactites and the walls smooth as if dug from hand. Curiously, this rock wasn't limestone like the rest of the cave, rather a sandy substance that resembled concrete.

"This has got to be manmade," Henry said. "Keep an eye out for arrowheads."

Carlos shook his head. "I'm not looking for no damn arrowheads. We'll come back with the proper gear." The tunnel extended straight in either direction, but he decided the best course would be uphill. Fairly soon they came to a branch, with two corridors leading off from the main one. Henry's comment about arrowheads gave Carlos an idea. He removed his buck knife and started carving an arrow into the wall.

"What's that for?" Henry asked.

"So we don't go in circles. Keeps us from doubling back on ourselves."

"Very clever."

"I got lost in a sewer once, chasing a gunman. After I found him, these arrows helped me resurface."

Henry regarded his friend for a moment, genuinely shocked.

Carlos grinned and chiseled out the last of the marker. "I did more than write traffic tickets, you know?"

"Well, obviously you ate donuts."

"I think I preferred the gunman's company. He spoke less."

As the two trudged on, they came to several more junctions - some branching off into three or four tunnels. Always they marked which tunnel they'd left and which they'd entered. Carlos wiped a layer of sweat from his brow.

"Have you noticed something?" he asked.

"What? You find an arrowhead?"

"No, the humidity's gone."

Henry sniffed the air. "Yeah, it is dry. Warmer too." He pulled off the sweater Carlos had given him and tied it around his waist.

Maybe that's what happens after a hurricane, Carlos thought, and then he swore. The candle had burned out and plunged them into blackness. He switched on his headlamp, but the battery was weak and so was its beam. Without light, they couldn't see the arrows he'd carved. They could end up wandering in circles forever.

"Wait, turn it off again." Henry sounded hopeful. "You see that?" Ahead through the darkness, Carlos could make out a pinpoint of light.

"Gracias adios." His exclamation echoed down the sandy corridor. Then another sound matched it; a deep rustling raced towards them out of the darkness.

"What the hell is that?" Henry asked. "It sounds like a bunch of people. Hello!" No reply came back, however, only the sound growing louder and more aggressive.

"That's not people," Carlos said, wincing at the obvious. He took off his pack and withdrew Mambo's sword. A high-pitched hiss filled the corridor as the clawing sound grew nearer. Carlos felt utterly defenseless with just this blade in his hand. He wished he had a firearm. Tossing the sword to the ground, he removed the tiny box Mambo had given him. He flipped open the lid, snatched the hollow marble inside, and stood with one fist poised over his head.

They could see no more than a few feet down the corridor due to the weakness of his headlamp. But they could tell from the sound that, whatever it was, it was almost upon them. And it sounded huge. Carlos felt dozens of tremors in the sand at his feet, and dust shook loose from the ceiling. Then the noise stopped.

The creature eyed them from no more than fifty feet away, Carlos was sure of it. The sand crackled as the beast leveraged its immense weight, scraping both walls at the same time. Carlos caught flickers of movement beyond his headlamp's beam – ghastly images of joints and claws. And then, as he heard the scuttle of renewed movement, he let loose with his hand and flung the marble straight into the darkness. It whizzed thru the dry air and shattered into a thousand pieces against a hidden target. An ear-piecing scream rose from the depths. These cries quickly faded, however, as the two men sprinted away. Carlos had left his pack behind but didn't care. All that mattered was getting away.

Soon, the light ahead completely engulfed them, and they staggered out of the tunnel into a white haze. On the foot where he'd lost his shoe, Carlos felt sand give way beneath his sock.

We must be somewhere near Henry's house, on the public beach, he figured. But Carlos didn't hear the surf, only wind. His eyes soon adjusted to the brightness, but it took his mind a little longer to register what he was seeing – sand dunes, and not just a few. Thousands of dunes stretched off in receding waves to the horizon. They were in a desert. The vista so shocked Carlos that he momentarily forgot something was chasing them.

Nothing like this existed on Cayman Brac. On its longest side, the island stretched only twelve miles across. Yet now he stared across what looked like hundreds of miles of sand. This had to be a dream – an especially lucid one. How far have we walked in the cave? Miles? No, there weren't any other islands like this nearby. Maybe the water has receded from the hurricane? No, that doesn't make any sense either. His mind spun through the possibilities, desperately seeking an answer. Then Carlos remembered something had chased them here, and he glanced back.

A dark hole marked the entrance to the tunnel they'd just left, emerging from the base of a mountain-sized dune. The cave looked empty, no sign of whatever had been after them. But Carlos didn't want to stick around and find out. He wished he hadn't lost his pack and the sword Mambo had given him.

"Let's move away from the tunnel."

"I'm hallucinating," Henry said. He knelt down and held his forehead with both hands. Red grains sparkled beneath him, too vivid to be a dream.

"No, I see it too," Carlos said. "We'll figure this out."

"Figure what out?" Henry eyes darted about rapidly. His breathing turned erratic. "We're dead. We're in Hell."

"Calm down. It's going to be fine. Look at me." He could see that his friend was shaking and crouched down next to him. "Look at me, Henry. Good, now deep breaths. It's going to be fine. This isn't Hell. Let's get away from the tunnel's entrance and regroup."

Carlos couldn't be sure this wasn't Hell, but he had to calm his friend. He'd lived through enough tough scrapes to know the danger in panicking. Henry's breathing slowed as he inhaled consciously.

"Good inhale, exhale." Carlos broke eye contact with him and focused over his friend's shoulder. A pole stuck out from the drifts beyond them, as if someone had jammed a walking staff there. Carlos stood up, streams of sand cascading off his clothes. He saw another pole; there were two side by side. Neither appeared wooden - instead they looked translucent, camouflaged against the sand with strange black knobs at their ends. The grains beneath the poles vibrated slightly and then lay still. Danger warnings lit up Carlos's head like fireworks. "Get up," he whispered.

Henry pushed him away. "Let me sit for a second."

"Just get up —" The sand exploded. Two massive claws pierced the evening sky. They thundered back down, sheets of dust swirling in their wake. Henry screamed. A hulking red crab, larger than anything they could ever imagine, lifted itself from the ground. Pincers swung out wildly. They tore through Carlos's shirt; a line of blood streaked across his chest. He stumbled backwards, pulling Henry out of the cloud that obscured the creature.

It paused, as if waiting for the air to clear, and then circled around them. Carlos forced himself to ignore Henry's screams. He had to focus, let his training kick in, and take stock of the situation before it overwhelmed them. First, he studied the crab as if it were an armed assailant.

This one was much larger than the crab that had killed Salty. Carlos gauged it to be about the size of his van, each leg as thick as a telephone pole. Elaborate tattoos covered its shell, radiating out from the creature's eyestalks. Even more striking were the gems encrusted amongst these designs: sapphires and emeralds, sparkling in the sunlight.

The crab studied him back, as if gauging whether they poised a threat. It preferred to move sideways, Carlos noted. He picked out its weak spots: the mouth and eyes. But he had no weapon.

Suddenly, the creature's whole body shuddered. Carlos had a feeling he knew why – it must have seen the claw he'd cut from Salty's killer. It was still tucked into his belt, clearly visible.

Oh God, had he killed its baby?

Carlos didn't have time to react. From its position only a few paces away, the creature shrieked angrily. Then it barreled at him full force, a primal stampede of anger. He heard a fierce yell, but not from Henry. It was a woman's voice.

A figure landed in the sand before them. She moved so fast Carlos just got an impression of dark hair and toned calves. Then the claw came down. The woman nimbly ducked to avoid it. Swirling back, she struck at the pincer with a wooden rod. The next blow splintered this weapon and sent her catapulting through the air. Instead of falling, she curled into a roll and unsheathed a sword that had been hidden behind her back.

"Run," she yelled. But Carlos wasn't about to leave someone at the creature's mercy, even if she looked like she could handle herself. The woman wore a Roman skirt with a red tunic that dangled sleeves – like something out of the comic books he used to read as a kid. A thin stone belt encircled her waist, and leather sandals wrapped around her feet. She brandished her sword calmly, eyes locked on the crab.

The creature roared and came at her with both claws surgically slicing the air. But she was ready for it. Her sword deflected both strikes. However, one of the pincers closed around her blade. The crab lifted her high into the air and tried to shake her loose. So the woman let go. She somersaulted forward onto the shell, landing in a crouch. After tossing back her dark hair, she removed a dagger from her ankle and struck.

The blade sliced through the crab's eye stalks, neatly severing them. Now blind, the creature screamed in pain. It fell backwards with a thundering crash, twisting in violent death throes until the legs curled back onto its shell. Meanwhile, the woman had vaulted over the crab, tucked like a gymnast, and landed softly in front of the two men, their mouths still agape.

"He's dead. And you're very lucky not to be." She sheathed her ankle dagger and walked over to retrieve her sword from the now still carcass. "He went into a blood frenzy. Not many survive that. Why have you ventured out this far?"

"Demons," was all Henry could say.

Carlos finally found his voice. "Where are we?"

The woman used her foot to pry open the crab's claw and pull her sword free.

"In trouble," she said, looking in their direction. Carlos noticed her green eyes for the first time. They peered out of an angular face, tanned by the sun and peppered with grains of sand. "You're outside the Kalfou. And fortunate to still draw breath."

She grinned and then, twisting her blade around, slid it into the scabbard across the small of her back. A few steps later and she was standing right in front of them. "What else would you expect here?" She eyed Henry's wetsuit with a mixture of curiosity and suspicion.

Am I hallucinating? Carlos thought. Who is this woman? And what is that thing she just killed? This has to be some sort of vivid dream.

The scratch across his chest said otherwise. The adrenalin faded into pain, and he winced. The wound at least was very real. It sent stabs of electricity through his nerves.

"Are we dead?" Carlos asked her, grimacing.

"You will be if I don't treat that wound."

"Demons," Henry repeated, his eyes large, pupils dilated. A far away expression had taken over his face. The woman examined Henry and then bit her lip.

She turned to Carlos. "Your friend's in shock," she said. Her voice carried a slight accent, however, it wasn't native to the Caymans, and Carlos couldn't place it. She spoke English but peppered her speech with foreign words. Language barrier or not, he had a thousand questions to ask.

"Is this the afterlife?" Carlos asked.

"You're not dead," she repeated. "Now stay still." She bent forward to inspect his injury.

Carlos wouldn't be so easily pacified. "Have you heard of the Brac?"

"Brac?" She gave him a quizzical look. "You're in shock too." With great care, she pulled back the bloody cloth around his chest. "It's not deep. Come on, I've made camp nearby. There's medicine there." She turned and started to walk up a dune. Carlos didn't follow.

"I'm sorry. We're not from here." He gestured back towards the tunnel. "We came from the caves."

The woman stopped.

"You were in there?" she asked, skeptical. Her eyes came to rest on the souvenir at his waist. "Where did you get that?" Before he could respond, she grabbed the claw and sniffed at its severed end. "It's fresh. You killed one?"

"Yes. It killed our dog," Carlos said.

"Salty," Henry added. His breathing had calmed down, replaced by a mask of fatigue. The woman ran her fingers along the claw.

"Are there many crabs that size?" Carlos asked, gesturing to the dead creature in the dust beyond them.

"The Sentry?" she asked. Putting her hands to her hips, she scrunched up her forehead. "What did you call him? Crabs?" She mouthed the word as if it were a foreign language. Then she carefully posed another question. "You're not from Ginen?"

"No," Carlos and Henry said in unison. That answer startled her.

"Is Ginen your country?" Carlos asked. "Where are you from?" She continued to silently stare at them, so he continued. "We need to return to our home. And seal off these caves to protect our people."

The woman shook her head. "As soon as night falls, fifty baka that size will swarm the area. We have little time."

Carlos' skin prickled as she spoke. He wanted to make sure he'd heard her correctly. "What did you call them?"

"Baka?"

The same word Mambo had used. Gurgling sounds erupted from the mouth of the crab behind them. Henry jumped reflexively.

"Don't worry. He's dead," she reassured them, pointing at her ankle dagger. "Poison blade."

It was too much to process. Baka. Deserts. Warrior amazons. Carlos took a deep breath. He wished he'd spoken to Mambo longer. She knew about this place, had tried to warn him and offer advice. What had she called it? Something about an island beneath the sea. Was this some kind of spirit world? His mind raced back through their conversation, trying to recall the details.

No. Stay in the moment, he thought. Look at what you have... a local to question, a guide. Considering she'd just saved them from certain death, for the moment that warranted their trust.

"I'm Carlos." He extended a hand. The woman took it and, pulling him close, touched her forehead with his. She smelled wonderful, a rustic spice he couldn't place, but its familiarity relaxed him. She repeated the greeting with Henry.

"Ayzili," she said, pointing to herself. "Now, we must hurry."

"I think we should go back," Henry said. He'd already taken a step towards the cave. Carlos put a hand on his shoulder.

"We will. Let's get some answers first."

Henry glanced backwards once more. "All right," he said at last.

Chapter 6

They followed Ayzili up the crest of a tall dune, which gave them a chance to take in their surroundings. The desert encompassed most of the horizon, but Carlos was comforted to see the ocean. It had been hidden by the ridge and was some distance off. But it was there. The dunes emptied directly into the water - like a beach with no end - just sea and sand for mile after mile.

Carlos had more questions for their guide, but they'd have to wait. Henry was hyperventilating again and needed his immediate attention.

"My Easter homily," Henry said, "all lies. Never had a pet Chinchilla."

"Well, that's certainly grounds for damnation."

Henry turned to him. "But you agree we're dead?"

"She said we're not."

"Maybe she's in denial too." Henry continued his litany of sins. "Didn't give up chocolate for Lent." He wiped the sweat from his nose. "Ogled Ms. Fullerton's cleavage."

"Who hasn't?" Carlos squinted into the sun as it died a red death over the ocean. "I don't know where we are," he said, "but it doesn't feel like the afterlife."

He considered sharing Mambo's words, then changed his mind. Henry was breathing hard. Right now, he just needed to calm down. Besides, Carlos had to gather more information before he put forth any theories. As crazy as it sounded, he had the feeling he'd been here before. He couldn't explain it, but the déjà vu was undeniable.

He spotted a silhouette on the coast, which broke him from his thoughts – an enormous fortress, walled in and spiked with minarets. It resembled an ornate sandcastle but impossibly huge.

"What's that?" he asked Ayzili. She locked eyes on the city and smiled.

"Ginen, of course."

Henry's jaw dropped when he saw the structure, and his face drained of color. Strange, thought Carlos. He's acting like he's seen this castle before; how is that possible? When Carlos asked if he was ok, Henry just mumbled something about drapos and would say no more.

The sandcastle seemed to bother him deeply, for he twisted the ring on his finger, engaged in quiet prayer. Carlos had seen him do this on several occasions. He too wanted answers but would go about it differently. Launching into the interview techniques he'd mastered over the years, Carlos began questioning Ayzili.

What is the date? What country is this? How many cities are there?

She ignored him, more worried about the fading light than answering questions. "Wait until we're safe," she said. "Then we can talk."

"I marked the cave's walls," he said. "I can lead us to a safe place underground."

Ayzili snorted. "There's nowhere safe in the Kalfou." She shielded her eyes from the sun and gazed over three low drifts in a sand bowl.

"This your camp?" Carlos asked. But Ayzili was already running down to one of the smaller dunes. Digging her fingers into the sand, she pulled back a flap and tossed it open. To the men's surprise, this was not a dune at all, but a tent dyed the color of the sand. "My Tapo," she said with a hint of pride and then disappeared beneath the canvas.

Henry eyed the opening. "My suit's damp from the ocean. I should let it dry."

"Not outside," Ayzili said. "Bring your clothes in."

"This is all I've got."

"Here." She tossed him out a blanket. "Wrap yourself in this."

As Henry peeled off his wetsuit, Carlos brushed the sand from his clothes and followed Ayzili inside. At once, he felt like he'd been here before, and he knew why. It looked exactly like Mambo's shed, the interior lined with the same drapo flags, only these were richer and more vibrant in color. Tiny red and gold threading filled the patchwork of squares. He examined the embroidery up close and saw that it depicted a battle between crabs and speared warriors. The men were easily outnumbered. Crustacean armies surrounded them in scenes eerily reminiscent of Custer's last stand.

Beneath these flags, blankets covered the floor. A cooking kit rested against one wall. And that was it. This was obviously a temporary dwelling.

"You call these drapos?" Carlos asked, pointing to the flags.

"Yes, from the Western Quarter of Ginen."

"Wow," Henry said, ducking inside with his sweater and makeshift toga. "Hell's stranger than I thought." Ayzili closed the flap behind him and lit three tiny candles. They soon filled the cramped interior with a cozy glow. After everyone had taken a seat, she handed over what looked like a dried-out lung. A cork in one end marked it as a water canteen, and Carlos took a healthy swig. " What —" Henry started but Ayzili pressed a finger to his lips.

"I want to hear your story but we must speak in whispers. We're near a baka hole and they own the night." The wind roared outside the tent to highlight her words, and the group fell silent. They could hear the sand blowing overhead. Lowering the water flask, Carlos noticed a streak of blood running down Ayzili's arm.

"You're injured."

She took stock of the wound – a jagged cut that ran across the copper skin of her shoulder. The baka had sliced through a row of tattooed lines there. "He got lucky," she said, shrugging.

Ayzili pulled up her legs and inched the stone belt from her hips. The carvings that graced its sides were nicked and scratched - likely from battle, Carlos guessed. This must be some kind of protective armor. She set the belt aside and laughed bitterly. "That baka had more jewels than kills to his credit, but he'd killed several."

"Several from Ginen?" Carlos asked. She studied his face to judge whether he was mocking her.

"Yes, you saw the veve on his back – one for each. Now tell me where you're from."

"A small island in the Caribbean, Cayman Brac. Our crabs are about this small." Carlos spread his hands apart for reference.

"And we eat them," Henry added, "not vice-versa." The joke meant he'd accepted their current predicament or at least mastered his fear. Be it heaven, Hell, or a shared hallucination, Henry was going to figure it out. That's what Carlos admired most about his friend - the ability to laugh in the face of hardship. It had helped him weather many storms. Thank God it survived the hurricane.

"Caribeyon?" Ayzili asked, butchering the pronunciation.

"We came through the cave," Carlos said. "Something, probably a baka, chased us out here. Tomorrow, when its safe, we'll retrace out steps, find my pack, and —"

"You cannot return that way," she interrupted. "It is the Kalfou, the crossroads, home of the baka. You're lucky to be alive. Now show me your injury." She took a cotton cloth, soaked it in water, and began to clean his wound. Bits of sand had congealed with the blood, and he grimaced as she scraped them free.

"But we can't stay here," Henry said. "We don't belong here."

"No one's entered a baka hole and lived to tell of it."

"Except us," Henry said.

Ayzili smirked. "So you say." She crushed some herbs beneath her thumb and forefinger and rubbed the garlicky juices into Carlos's chest. Then she applied a fresh cloth and cinched it tight. Satisfied with her first aid, Ayzili bent her arm and repeated the procedure on her shoulder.

When she'd finished, she reached for her cooking kit and started to assemble a small stove. This consisted of a metal framework in which she set one of the candles. Above the flame, she affixed an earthen pot - the whole contraption now reminding Carlos of a fondue kit.

He looked up from the cookware to study her expression. Carlos was fairly good at reading people, a skill he'd perfected during countless eyewitness interviews. From her calm demeanor, he felt Ayzili had made up her mind about them – that they were crazy, crazy but harmless. Now it was her turn to answer some questions.

"You've never heard of the Caymans?" Carlos began. It was soon apparent she lacked even the most basic understanding of Caribbean geography.

"I don't understand. Your speech is difficult," she said, emptying most of the water into the pot.

"Ginen, is that the nearest city?" Carlos asked.

"Yes, and that is the only one. The baka have destroyed all others. Give me the claw." Carlos obliged and watched as she cracked open the shell, jerked the tender parts free of the bone, and tossed them into the pot.

"Can't the baka smell that?" Henry asked, inhaling the sweet aroma of the crabmeat. His stomach growled in anticipation. Ayzili yawned, covered the soup, and sat back to let it boil.

"They cannot," she said simply.

But Henry didn't sound convinced. "How many are out there?"

"Many thousands." Then she smiled. "But not too many for me to kill. They hide their numbers beneath the sand." She placed the shell fragments from the claw into a leather pouch.

"So we'll need weapons before going back," Carlos said.

She regarded him with an amused expression. "You wish to die?" Still smirking, she tossed a pinch of herbs into the soup.

"No, but we do need to get home."

"I will take you to Ginen tomorrow. You'll need to visit the falls to..." she hesitated, then stared at Carlos' chest and said, "...mend your wound."

"I think I'll be fine."

"A baka's injuries aren't to be ignored. They'll eat away at you." She took the bowl from the stove and offered it to Carlos. "Drink. You'll need your strength."

The meal tasted delicious but unlike any crab soup Carlos had ever eaten. The flavors were richer and heartier for one thing, like a gumbo roux. And the spices burnt his lips.

He considered their options. They could retrace their steps through the tunnel tomorrow, with luck avoiding another baka encounter. Or they could follow Ayzili to this place Ginen and arm themselves first. Since they currently lacked weapons, the latter option seemed the obvious choice.

"We'll go with you to Ginen tomorrow," Carlos said, "but we can't stay." He made eye contact with Henry, assuring him that this was the best course of action. Henry's eyes tightened, thoroughly unconvinced. No sense sheltering him any longer, Carlos thought. He had a hunch about this place, and they needed to know the truth, regardless of the spiritual implications.

"Ayzili, do you know someone named Mambo Lalin?" he asked.

She shook her head. "I know several Mambos, but no Lalin."

"Your people in Ginen —"

"They're not my people anymore," she said sternly.

"Well," Carlos tried to verbalize the question that had been nagging him for hours. "Do all of you practice —" But before he could finish, Ayzili cupped a hand over his mouth. She mouthed the word "Baka" and blew out the tea candles. No one moved.

The rumble of heavy impacts was clearly audible amidst the wind outside – something was crawling quite near the Tapo. They heard the sand shift as long legs sunk deep into the drifts and lifted out again. Gradually the sound faded into the distance, but no one dared speak.

Ayzili quietly collected the cooking gear and stowed it in a corner of the tent. Then she lay down between the two men, her dagger noticeably clutched across her chest. Whether this served as protection against the baka or her new guests, Carlos couldn't be sure.

He glanced at Henry, but his friend had already bunched up a blanket into a makeshift pillow and was beginning to snore. It wouldn't be so easy for Carlos. Countless stakeouts had trained his body to resist sleep. So he stretched out for appearances' sake and stared up at the weavings on the ceiling. They glowed back eerily, illuminated by the moonlight overhead. These images were skillfully rendered, an epic battle between man and crab. He noticed that the crabs were tearing their captives apart; it was obvious who was winning. Above this scene had been stitched a portrait of a woman. Carlos recognized this image at least – the Virgin Mary, but with a dagger piercing her heart.

He'd seen this before. And the saintly icon confirmed a suspicion he held about Ayzili - at least about her beliefs.

When Europeans first came to the Caribbean they banned their slaves from practicing African religions. So the slaves used Catholic saints to cover for the older spirits of their homeland. Mix in the native Indian cultures and this spiritual gumbo eventually created new religions such as Voodoo and Santeria.

The Madonna with a blade through her heart was a popular Voodoo spirit, protector of children or something like that. His ex-wife had explained all this to him after she'd built a tiny altar in their home. She'd decorated it with candles that prominently featured this Saint. And now here it was again, the exact same icon stitched all over the tent.

Could Ayzili be part of some lost voodoo society?

When he thought for sure she'd fallen asleep, Carlos turned towards her. Face to face, Ayzili's features were all the more striking: a chiseled face of hardened beauty with a scar rising from one cheek.

Her eyes flashed open. Seas of green swirled about her pupils so mesmerizing, he could not look away.

"When you entered the crossroads," she whispered. "Did you see him?"

“Did I see who?”

“Papa Legba,” she asked.

“Who’s that?”

“Papa Legba, the old man with a crutch. Did you see him?”

“No, I didn’t see anyone,” Carlos answered. Her face flashed disappointment, then settled into resignation.

“I thought so.” She closed her eyes. Carlos felt her wince and lie still. Minutes later, her free arm fell across his chest. Carlos hadn’t been this close to a woman since his wife left him, and his adrenalin surged. He’d never fall asleep now.

Where ever I am, it’s definitely not Hell, he thought.

Chapter 7

The first few seconds after Carlos awoke, he thought he was back home, on the island of Cayman Brac. He heard the roar of waves, could almost see the rafters of the humble shack he'd rented, and then his eyes focused. Sunlight burnt off the mists of sleep.

"Wake up, Carlos. I think she wants to get moving." Henry crouched over him, wearing his makeshift toga like some middle-aged frat boy. "The heat's gonna be brutal soon."

Carlos leaned up and saw that most of the tent had already been disassembled. Ayzili knelt some distance away with a long sheet in her hands. The silk rippled wildly in the wind, creating the ocean-like sounds he had heard earlier. She nimbly twisted her hands through the fabric and folded the sheet into a tight square, tucking it away into a canvas pack. Soon she'd broken down the entire campsite, packed it away, and heaved the assemblage onto her shoulders. If the weight bothered her, she didn't show it.

"Your wound, does it hurt?" she asked, hiking up to him.

"No, I can walk. What should I carry?"

"Nothing. We must get to Ginen before mid-day." And with that she swung around and began ascending the nearest dune. Carlos started to follow when he noticed that Henry wasn't moving.

"Carlos, I'm going back to the tunnel." No sign of panic strained Henry's voice, just a determined finality. He had made up his mind.

"We will, but first let's get something to defend ourselves." Carlos motioned up the dune.

"No, I need to go back now. I can't stay here."

Ayzili dropped her pack to the sand and stomped down the hill. "Your friend's wasting time."

"I'm sorry. I can't do this." Henry shook his head, "We don't belong here."

"You'd prefer a baka's belly?" Ayzili asked.

Henry swallowed. "Let's go, before things get worse."

"You want to enter the baka's nest? Are you mad?" Ayzili grabbed Henry roughly by the shoulder and shook him until Carlos intervened.

"Everyone, just calm down." He took a deep breath. "What are the chances we'd encounter another baka down there?"

Ayzili smiled. Finally she said, "Let me show you." Then without further explanation, she stormed off toward the tunnel, the two men trailing warily. Approaching the entrance, she dropped to her knees and proceeded the remaining distance up the dune on her stomach.

"Keep your heads down," she ordered, peering over the crest.

The tunnel's entrance looked exactly as when they'd first encountered it. Exactly, the same.

"Where'd the crab's body go?" Henry asked.

Ayzili shushed him and gestured towards the sandy basin. If it weren't for the shadows Carlos might have missed them: eyestalks. Several dozen rods now emerged from the sand like the stakes of a dead vineyard. A few appeared equal in height to his chest. He shuddered to think the size of the creatures hidden beneath them.

"You still want to go down there?" Ayzili asked.

* * *

Even though she carried the pack, Ayzili maintained a steady lead on the two men, who quickly dropped behind and ended up following her tracks. Obviously, she intended to win her race with the sun. Carlos could have matched her pace but wanted to speak with his friend alone.

"We're being tested," Henry said once she was out of earshot.

"How do you mean?"

"Demon crabs, beautiful women." He motioned towards Ayzili. "I was too bold in surfing that hurricane. Took it for granted the Lord'll protect me. And now he's testing my faith. That's what this place is —"

"Uh huh. Then why am I here?"

"I don't know," He patted Carlos stomach. "Maybe he thought you could use 40 days in the wilderness."

Carlos ignored the jab at his gut. "Do you remember dying?" he asked. "See a white light?" He shrugged. "Me neither. This isn't purgatory."

"No," Henry stopped to catch his breath, "it's Mambo's superstitions come to life. The last flag she gave me had a sandcastle on it. One exactly like that." He gestured wildly to the structure in the distance. "Mambo's working with that devil woman to take our souls." Henry's face cracked as he said it. That was a sentence he never thought he'd utter. He couldn't help but laugh.

"When did you get all fire and brimstone, father?" Carlos knew Henry was scrambling to find a spiritual foothold, to make sense of it all. It was best to just let him vent.

"Seriously, you saw the Virgin Mary stitched into her tent? Notice the knife in her heart?" Henry's eyes widened. "Devil worship."

"That's not devil worship." Carlos sighed. "It's the symbol for a voodoo spirit. So's this medallion Mambo gave me." He held it up for Henry to see. "Even Naomi had a few icons like this. They're very common."

Henry shook his head. "Your wife's into that?"

"She's not my wife anymore, Padre. And it's no big deal. Just calm down."

"You're using your cop voice." Henry folded his arms. "You know, there could be spiritual consequences for us."

"You figure that out. I'll focus on getting us home."

"Spiritual consequences," Henry repeated. He'd fallen back into the safety blanket of Catholic dogma. That's where he always goes when he gets flustered, Carlos thought. But he knew his friend. He'd open up soon.

"Let's just relax. If we play along, there may be a way...to get her to guide us back through the caves. She's looking for something."

A long shot to be sure, but sharing his plan with Henry might lift his friend's mood. So Carlos continued, "In these folk religions, there's a bunch of spirits. Well, Ayzili mentioned one to me last night; she asked if I'd seen him down there."

"You spoke after we went to sleep? Henry scrunched his brow.

"Yeah, she asked about this spirit named Papa Legba. Mambo always invokes his name when she's lost something —"

"Papa Legba doesn't exist," Ayzili said. "None of them do." She was only a few paces away. The two men hadn't heard her approach and weren't sure how much she'd overheard. They stood there awkwardly as she continued, "But that's what I thought about people living beyond Ginen. And yet, here you are. So I'm not certain of much anymore." She sized them up for several moments before hefting the weight of her pack and trudging on through the sand.

So much for that plan, Carlos thought. Evidently Ayzili wasn't as religious as they'd assumed. He glanced at Henry, who just shrugged. She certainly wasn't acting like a temptress sent by the devil to test their faith.

Besides, Carlos knew what a real test of faith was. And after his failure in Miami, he didn't think God would try again.

* * *

Although the sun had crested high above them and was making good progress on its downward trek, the temperature seemed only to increase. Carlos couldn't tell which was hotter – the sun above or the sand below. Ayzili had given him an oily cream to rub over his skin, but he could already feel the sunburns. He'd also developed a headache, the first sign of dehydration. Henry fared no better. He propped up his glasses, wiped the sweat from his eyes, and grumbled something under his breath about spiritual consequences.

Carlos ignored his friend's complaints. He wanted to learn more about the people of Ginen before they arrived there. But every time he brought it up, Ayzili fell silent. They had hit a nerve with her, so rather than pushing the issue, he focused on their destination ahead.

As he stared at the walled city his mind drifted back to Miami's South Beach. Memories of that place wavered before him like a mirage on the horizon. His wife Naomi snored peacefully in her folding chair beneath the umbrella. He crouched next to her, packing wet sand into a bucket, molding it, and emptying the contents out for his daughter, Violet.

'You need some more zinc for your nose," he told her. She ignored his parenting and continued to work on the sandcastle. They had only completed half the structure, and he doubted they would finish before the tide rose. This had been the last moment they'd spent together as a family, a normal family. He remembered his daughter garnishing the towers with strands of seaweed. She was probably imagining what it would be like to live in a castle made of sand. Well, he was about to find out.

The distances were deceptive. He had thought they'd have reached the walled city long ago. But they still had some distance to cross. The stucco metropolis rose in layers like a wedding cake before them.

Gradually, he began to make out detail in the structures rising beyond its walls. The city was a dense collection of balconies, staircases, and adobe blocks, all interwoven into a tangled maze. Two towers dominated the architecture, like twin lighthouses.

Carlos was so distracted by the view, he almost collided with a huge, white boulder. He took a step back. It wasn't a boulder.

"The skeleton of a baka?" he asked.

Ayzili nodded. "From a battle long ago." The sun had long since bleached the bones of color, yet they still appeared horrifyingly alive.

Carlos shivered. "Where's the shell?"

"The sand wore it away. This is all that remains." Ayzili continued her stride. A wooden post rose from one of the skull's eye sockets with a red flag snapping atop its mast. Ayzili rapped her fingers against the pole as she passed.

Henry gasped. Below them lay a hundred more crab skeletons of varying sizes, each with its own flag. They were scattered amongst the low dunes, extending all the way to the base of the city. Ayzili pointed to an unusual cluster of house-sized boulders nearby.

"I need to stow my pack. Then I'll walk you into the city." She jogged to a crack in the rocks and slipped through the opening.

Carlos and Henry followed her, squeezing through the tight space, which widened into a chamber carved from the rock. A grated skylight illuminated the room from above and caught floating particles in its beams.

"This is my home," Ayzili said.

The cave was obviously a permanent residence. Silk draped the walls and divided the main living area from a small kitchen off to the side. Ayzili dumped her pack here and then scraped two rocks together over a rock pedestal. A tiny fire sprung to life. She tossed the rocks away and reached for a bladder hanging from a hook. Uncorking it, she offered them each some water.

"You don't live in the city?" Carlos asked.

"Not anymore...I used to."

"Can't the baka get in?" Henry glanced warily back at the entrance.

"The small ones can," she gestured to the wall over her shoulder, on which hung a dozen tiny crab skeletons. "A legion of baka tried to wait me out once; they camped outside for almost a week." She swallowed a mouthful of water. "My arrows got them eventually." When she lifted one of the skeletons mounted to the wall, a beam of light shot out from behind it. A hole had been drilled through the rock just large enough for the shaft of an arrow. "I can handle my own."

"I can see that," Carlos said, finishing his survey of the interior. "But why do you live out here?"

"I choose to," she said cryptically. He decided to drop the subject.

Meanwhile, Henry had found a wall free of crab skeletons – a portrait of a man and young boy hung there. He reached out and felt the fabric.

"Is this your family?" he asked.

Ayzili's frown returned. Evidently, Henry had touched upon another sore spot. Carlos wondered if the baka had killed them. Or maybe they'd just been separated. If they were to get any more information out of her, they'd have to tread more carefully.

Ayzili just ignored Henry's question and instead said, "Hand me one of those rods." Carlos noticed a set of thin needles stretching across the fire she'd lit. Each had a wooden handle at its end.

"What are they for?" Henry asked, nervously.

"I have to mark the baka kill," Ayzili said. She took the wire from Carlos and pulled up her sleeve, revealing once more the row of tattooed lines that curled up her arm. With great care, she dipped the wire into an ink jar and then pressed it into her flesh. Henry had to look away.

"I hate needles," he said.

Ayzili laughed. "Yet you'll walk into the Kalfou unarmed?"

Sensing her anger building up, Carlos changed the subject again. "Who's in charge of Ginen?" he asked.

"The council of elders. They set laws and pass judgment."

"Can we speak to this council?"

"You can try. But the high priesthood holds many seats. And they're not to be trusted." Traces of resentment tainted her voice. Stay away from local politics, Carlos told himself. Talking with this woman was like navigating a minefield. He sensed their constant questions were already fraying her nerves. Ayzili finished inking her tattoo and set down the needle.

"I'd like to meet them today, this council," Carlos said.

"It's possible. But if we don't leave now, we'll have to spend the night here. And I'm low on supplies." She grabbed a smaller pack and led them outside. Carlos made note of the sun's position. They still had several hours before nightfall. Why the rush?

Before long they arrived at the city wall. A large pair of wooden gates, encrusted with barnacles, barred their path. Carlos took a deep breath and smelled the salt in the air. The ocean had to be quite close. Ayzili waved towards the top of the wall, where presumably someone was watching. All Carlos could see were the faces of gargoyles - wicked fish mouths lined with teeth.

"Can the baka climb these walls?" he asked.

"No," Ayzili said. "They find other ways in."

He wanted to ask her what she meant by this but was interrupted by a grinding noise, as if immense gears were churning beyond the doors. With a deep shudder, they creaked open wide enough to allow the three to enter. Cautiously, he and Henry followed their guide into the city of Ginen.

Chapter 8

As the doors rolled away, Carlos heard a flutter of wings. A chicken hurried to flee their path, flapping across the road ahead. It was almost crushed to death by a bull-drawn cart painted in hues of gold. Ayzili waved at its passengers: tan men and women wrapped in swaths of fabric as colorful as their ride.

They returned the gesture as their cart rumbled up a nearby street. The neighborhood slightly resembled a Moroccan village, Carlos thought, all stucco with painted murals and doorways. The illusion would've been complete were in not for a Gothic Cathedral that loomed in the distance. It was too much to take in at once.

"My God," said Henry. Carlos nodded, equally dumbstruck. He sidestepped to let a man carrying earthenware jugs pass into a crowd full of sarong-wrapped women. It felt like they'd stepped into the pages of the Old Testament.

"How many people live here?" he asked, his nostrils stinging with the smells of burnt charcoal and mango.

Before Ayzili could answer, a scrawny youth dressed in purple robes ran up to them. He looked in his early twenties with a shaven head that gave him a monk-like appearance. The man hesitated when he saw Carlos and Henry. Then he turned his attention to Ayzili.

"Zui, what's your hurry?" she asked.

"A rel's been called, from the Northern Quarter. Moro's house."

Ayzili's eyes widened. She set off immediately in a dead sprint. With little choice, Carlos and Henry hurried behind her. They raced through alleys and up winding stairs in a blind dash to keep up.

The people of Ginen turned to stare as they rushed past. Carlos couldn't tell if it was because of their dress or their speed. Either way, he hoped they were almost there. Henry had fallen behind and was forced to pull up his blanket like a gown. He'd already tripped a number of times. Ayzili, however, only quickened her pace. As they continued through the streets, a faint cry rose in the distance.

"What's that sound?" Carlos asked.

Ayzili frowned. "A rel," she said simply. The sound grew in volume the farther they traveled, until it became almost a scream. Then it abruptly stopped. They'd arrived at a smoky marketplace - claustrophobic, dimly lit, and filled with more merchants than customers. Booths of various wares bordered each side of the narrow street.

Ayzili ducked under a stand of cow hides and continued through an archway. They emerged into a courtyard where a sizable crowd had gathered. A dozen men, all armed to the teeth with massive sabers, blocked the entrance to the house beyond them.

Ayzili went straight to the tallest. "Hungar, where is she?"

The man named Hungar was huge, his shirt straining beneath the flex of powerful muscles. A dark mustache and several scars ripped across his face. With a pair of barbells, he could've easily passed for a 19th century strongman. This guy's the voice of authority here, Carlos thought. His stance said so. But as Hungar's glower fell upon Ayzili, the toughness faded. His eyes fell to the ground.

"She's gone," he said.

"No, we can still take her to the falls. Sasha's young —" She tried to struggle pass him, but he blocked her with one muscled arm.

"She's been dead for hours." Ayzili was hyperventilating now, and Hungar had trouble restraining her. "The baka killed her," Hungar said, his eyes tearing.

"Let me go. I want to see her." She shoved his arm back violently and had drawn her sword before anyone could react.

"The baka's long gone. Jell's performing the desounen."

This must be some kind of funeral rite, Carlos guessed, and the rel, a mourning cry. He could hear chanting and a rattle's shake from inside the house. For a moment, he worried Ayzili might strike this huge man blocking her path, but at last Hungar moved aside, revealing a small doorway in the wall. Gripping her weapon, Ayzili walked to the entrance. Her sword fell to the dirt. Carlos peered over her slumped shoulders.

The inside of the house was spartan, only a scattering of wooden chairs and tables. At its center, a straw mat had been unrolled, and on top of that rested the body of a young girl, no older then twelve. Crimson soaked through the sheet draping her wounds. Above the body, a priest in satin robes shook his rattle as he preformed the death rites. But it was the girl's face that drew Carlos's attention.

Her image burned into his mind. He felt a rush of emotion and in a flash the young girl vanished. In her place he saw his own daughter, Violet. She also lay still, not breathing. The life had drained from her eyes. Carlos gasped and tried to shake the vision. He couldn't bear to see this again. For so long he had tried to forget it. As if obeying his thoughts, the image faded back into the stranger's room again.

The priest waved his hands for them to leave. So, Ayzili stepped away from the doorway and spoke to the man named Hungar once more.

"Does her father know?" she asked.

"He's out on expedition." Hungar eyed Carlos and Henry suspiciously. "Who are these two?"

"I found them out by the crescent hole. I think the baka drove them mad."

"Who are you? Why are you dressed like that?" Hungar asked. The other warriors encircled them. Carlos exhaled forcefully and noticed he was sweating. The vision of his daughter had rattled him, but this was no time to loose his composure.

"We're not from Ginen," he began slowly.

"You're from the outer territories?" The young man who had met them at the gate seemed hopeful.

"That's not possible," Hungar said grimly. "There are no more survivors."

“We’re strangers from far away,” Carlos said. He tried to keep his voice calm and even. ”We need to get home. We have to warn our people about the baka. Can you help us return there?”

“They said they came through the Kalfou,” Ayzili said. “They’ve been attacked by the baka. Clearly, they’re not well.”

Hungar eyed the bandage across Carlo’s chest. Then he reached out and grabbed the wetsuit Henry had tied around his waist. “There’s black magic here. Lock them up.” He tossed the wetsuit to one of his men.

Ayzili stepped forward and shouted at Hungar. “You superstitious fool! You can’t do that.”

The guards grabbed Carlos and Henry roughly by the neck, but she cast them a look and they quickly let go. “These men aren’t dangerous,” she continued. “They’ve been with me the whole time. They’re in shock and need rest.”

Hungar shook his head and motioned for his men to escort them away.

“Wait.” Carlos said, his heart rate finally slowing. He knew he was losing control of the situation, yet all he could think about was his daughter. Keep it together, he thought. “If we’re being charged with a crime,” he said. “I want to know what it is.”

“You might be a sorcerer,” Hungar said flatly, “letting the baka into our city.”

“Ayzili can vouch for us,” Carlos said. “If we were allied with the baka, why they’d try to kill us?” Hungar scoffed at this notion and turned away.

Ayzili ran forward to confront him. She leaned over his ear. "Look, I know you feel you must do something to save face. But just because you can't secure this city, doesn't give you the right to imprison two very sick men."

Henry shook his head. "Who's sick?"

Hungar stared directly into Ayzili's fiery eyes. "You have no voice here anymore." He motioned to his guards. "Take them."

Carlos felt a strong push towards the archway leading back to the marketplace.

"Wait, let us speak to the high council first," he said. "We can help each other." But the guards had already grabbed him by the arm.

"Don't resist. I'll come for you," Ayzili yelled as they were marched away.

* * *

Carlos could sense figures staring at them from the curved windows they hurried past. Occasionally, he caught a glimpse of a family eating supper or an old woman reading. It seemed they were taking a back way so as not to draw attention - for the alleys kept getting narrower. The labyrinth of streets reminded him of his honeymoon in Rome, minus the tourist boutiques.

Are we destined for some medieval dungeon? By now, Carlos had certainly questioned the wisdom of entering the city. And Henry was kind enough not to rub it in. But something else occupied his mind right now.

Over the past year Carlos had thought of his daughter often, everyday in fact, but he'd never had a vision like the one he'd just witnessed.

It had been frighteningly real. And it had opened the floodgates, releasing waves of suppressed emotion.

"Are you ok?" Henry asked.

"Yeah..." Carlos lied and then said, "that girl was Violet's age." He didn't need to explain further.

"Quiet," one of the guards barked. Carlos returned to examining the streets. Soon they came to a crossroads and had to stop. A cart, overloaded with lamps, blocked their path.

"Move this thing," ordered one of the guards. A gnomish man in a burlap vest gave them a nasty look as he wheeled to one side, the lamps in his cart clinking together musically like an off key wind chime. In one hand, he held a flickering torch, which cast reflected light onto his glass menagerie.

"Move yourself," the gnomish man cursed under his breath. 'I've got half the city left to light." He returned to igniting the lanterns along a wall. A trail of glowing lamps revealed the direction he'd already traveled. Carlos couldn't tell if his anger was directed at him or Hungar's men.

Either way, the guards didn't pay any notice. They returned to their forced march, quietly talking amongst themselves. Now that they were out of earshot of Hungar, the guards had loosened up noticeably. Carlos and Henry soon fell to the back of the pack, a younger guard assigned to watch them. The man caught sight of Carlos's wristwatch.

"It tells me the time," Carlos whispered, pulling up his sleeve.

"The time?" The guard arched an eyebrow.

"The hour of the day," Carlos said. "See the numbers?" He pressed a side button, illuminating the watch's face. The guard drew in his breath. Carlos had the man's attention; now it was just a matter of reeling him in. He unclasped the watch. "I need to speak to a council member in private. Can you arrange that?"

The guard glanced around to see if any of the other guards had overheard them. "Possibly," he said quickly.

Carlos slipped him the timepiece. "It's urgent."

The guard pocketed the bribe and looked straight ahead. "I'll see what I can do," he said. Carlos smiled.

Right now they needed all the allies they could get. He had little faith Ayzili would free them from imprisonment. They couldn't count on that. For all he knew, they'd be locked away indefinitely with no hope of a trial. By the wrinkles in Henry's forehead, Carlos knew his friend was thinking the same thing.

The maze of alleys and passageways ended abruptly in a dead end flanked by high walls. That meant they had some altitude to climb. From their desert trek, Carlos remembered that part of Ginen rose in layers like a wedding cake. How far up will we climb? An unassuming doorway in the wall led them to a spiral staircase. One of the guards lit a torch and led the way.

"I think my legs are going to give out," Henry said after a few twists.

"Keeping going," ordered one of the guards.

"I'm not exactly dressed for this." Henry motioned to the blanket wrapped around him like a toga. The guard responded by shoving him forward.

The staircase wasn't close to ending and, after a few minutes, Carlos felt like it might even be spinning against them - a corkscrew plunging into an invisible wine bottle. They trudged on in silence, emerging at last into a tiny cell. It was unremarkable save for single window. Carlos tried to make eye contact with the younger guard, but the man avoided his gaze. The door shut firmly behind them, and bolts slid into place. Henry yanked at his blanket, which had gotten stuck in the door crack.

"You think he'll help us?" he asked.

"I don't know, but we can't count on it." Carlos' mind was already spinning the possibilities. They wouldn't last long here without food or water, and he couldn't assume the guards would bring them any. He sized up the door. Escaping that way would be tricky. Perhaps they could jimmy the hinges.

He decided to wait a while before trying. Some of the guards may have hung around outside. "Thanks," he said, almost as an afterthought.

"For what?" Henry moved to the window, stumbling over his blanket as he walked.

"For not rubbing it in...about entering the city. It was a bad idea."

"Well, I'm the one who went surfing in a hurricane, so I can't talk."

Carlos smiled and joined his friend by the window. It quickly became clear how high they'd climbed. Beyond the window, a sheer drop plunged to the streets far below. He guessed they were in a tower. The view distracted him from his escape plans. "That's some high tide."

This was an understatement. The ocean had wrapped itself around the outer walls of the city, cutting Ginen off from the dunes a short distance away and turning the entire metropolis into an island. An island beneath the sea.

He wouldn't keep his friend in the dark any longer. The time had come to tell Henry everything about his conversation with Mambo.

"She did know about this place," Carlos began. He paced back and forth, recounting each detail Mambo had told him, including her advice on finding the evil men who dealt with the baka. Henry settled into a corner of the cell and wrapped himself in the blanket like Mother Teresa, absorbing it all without interrupting. Then he pinched the bridge of his nose and took a deep breath.

"Look," he said, "I won't pretend to know what this place is anymore. But the Lord guided us here for a reason."

Carlos remained silent, glad Henry had finally acknowledged they might not be in purgatory. That would make it easier for him to accept what he was about to say. Henry beat him to it. "I know what you're thinking, and it's not that simple."

"A little girl was killed," Carlos said.

Henry recognized the look in his friend's eyes. "This isn't Miami, Carl."

"Someone led the baka to her."

"How do you know that?" Henry asked.

Carlos shrugged. "A hunch."

"They're not going to let you investigate." Henry pointed towards the locked door for emphasis. "They think we helped the creatures."

It wasn't like Henry to sweat the details. Carlos waited patiently for Henry to state his real concern. He didn't have to wait long. Henry let out a defeated sigh. "If cracking this case is our purpose here, then why'd the Good Lord bring me? I solve crosswords, not murders."

"Don't know," Carlos said. "I stopped asking 'why', years ago." Carlos didn't want to probe his reasons any deeper, so instead he gazed out at the city and tried to absorb the layout. They had to find someone in power – someone that would listen to them. But Henry wouldn't be so easily pacified.

"This is about Violet, isn't it?" he asked softly.

"I don't know," Carlos answered. He couldn't deny the vision of his daughter had affected him. But he also felt a gut sense of purpose. This was just something he had to do. A little girl had been killed. He'd find the person responsible before another child was hurt. It was that simple.

Henry sighed. "So what's our plan?"

Carlos smiled. He couldn't do this without Henry and was thankful his friend stood by his side. "First we find those in power and plead our case. We need access."

"Yes, excellent plan. But hard to do while we're locked up. And that Hungar fellow didn't seem very accommodating."

They both lapsed into thought and stared out at the cityscape, a dense patchwork of rooftops and alleyways. The massive Cathedral dominated the scene, like a paperweight resting atop an Escher drawing.

The structure contained flying buttresses, stained glass, and a gothic-style architecture. But beyond that, it was unlike any church Carlos had ever seen. Although its arms formed the classic shape of a cross, each one extended an equal length - with a single tower sprouting from their intersection. From a distance, it resembled a giant tree stump with four roots.

"Crux immissa quadrata," Henry said. "The shape's a Greek cross. Unusual for a Cathedral."

"Ayzili said the high priesthood holds a lot of power. If we could just get word out to them." He did remember her warning that the high priesthood couldn't be trusted. However, Ayzili didn't seem to trust anyone, and they needed to speak with someone in authority.

A sound of gunfire broke their attention from the Cathedral. The two men leaned out the window and squinted into the sunset. A mixture of drums and chanting accompanied the sound. Far below they saw a gathering crowd – a boisterous parade marching down the street. Some in the procession blew horns as they walked. Others beat drums or chanted in time to the rhythm. The gunshot sounds came from a man leading the group with a long whip, which he cracked occasionally into the air.

"Some kind of festival," said Henry.

"Probably trying to rid the city of those baka creatures." Carlos returned to the door. The hinges were thick and coated in rust, which would make prying them off difficult, especially since they had nothing to use for leverage. What he wouldn't give for a crowbar.

Actually, right now he'd prefer some aloe for his sunburn. It stung something fierce.

"You think these priests will help us?" Henry asked. "What if they're as superstitious as Mambo?"

"Then we use that to our advantage." Carlos pried at the hinges with his fingers, but they wouldn't budge. So he unfastened his belt and wrapped it around the metal. "Mambo believes the world's filled with these spirits; she calls them lwa. Each one's unique."

He was about to about to compare them to Catholic saints but decided Henry wasn't ready to hear that, and so he continued, "You have to honor these spirits because they can influence the events in your life. Good or bad. And everyone has their own protective spirit, like a guardian angel." He doubled the belt around his palm and pressed a foot against the door. "Mambo says hers sits on her head. And...that's really all I know..."

That wasn't entirely true. His wife had taught him a good deal more, but he didn't see any reason to drag Naomi into this. With a sudden jerk, Carlos pulled back on his belt. Bits of rust scraped off the hinges, but the metal itself remained in place.

"Mambo's a character all right." Henry crossed his arms. "She tried to convert you, eh?"

Carlos wasn't about to engage in religious debate. Instead he dropped the belt and leaned against the doorframe. The leather had bit into his skin. "It wasn't Sunday school," he said. "I was just stocking groceries."

From down in the streets, the chanting of the parade grew louder. Hurrying back to the window, they saw that the group had come to an intersection and appeared to be performing some ritual. Their leader was drawing elaborate patterns in the sand. Around him, the crowd had swelled in number – it seemed as if the whole city were there.

However, another noise drew the men's attention back inside the cell. Someone was unlocking the door's bolts. It swung open, a guard stepped aside, and Ayzili entered the room. The young monk they'd met at the gates followed directly behind her, clutching a stack of robes and sandals.

"I've spoken to the council elders," Ayzili said. "I told them you were with me at the time of the girl's attack. They agreed you couldn't be involved. So, you've been released into my custody."

Carlos exhaled in relief, "Can we speak with these elders?"

"In good time." Her eyes flashed concern as she studied his features. "First we must visit the falls. You're ill."

The monk stepped forward. "I'm Zui. The gardens you'll visit are a sacred place. Please change into these robes."

"Thank Goodness," Henry said, "my toga was starting to chafe something terrible."

Chapter 9

The prison guards left them to travel alone. Soon they'd descended a wider set of stairs that seemed to plunge on forever – much farther than they'd climbed. Carlos thought they might be below sea level when they finally emerged into a curving chamber, much like the lobby of a concert theatre. He had thanked Ayzili for freeing them and then asked how she did it so quickly.

"I know the head of the council," she said with a mischievous grin.

"In the Biblical sense?" Henry asked, but Carlos punched him in the shoulder before he could elaborate.

"He's a reasonable man," Ayzili continued, "yet the high priesthood undercuts his power. They don't trust him." She made a point of looking at Zui as she said this, but he avoided her gaze.

"Who leads the priesthood then?" Carlos asked, trying to grasp the politics.

"A man named Sarn." She let an edge of contempt creep into her voice. "If you're fortunate, we won't cross paths tonight."

Zui explained, "Our order tends the gardens. We live in the monastery."

"Not the Cathedral?" Henry asked.

Ayzili shook her head. "No, that belongs to everyone." She paused, realizing how little these strangers knew. "Years ago the high priesthood broke ranks with the other priests of Ginen. They wanted to force their religious laws on the people. When that didn't happen, they cloistered up here, declaring themselves protectors of the gardens."

"It's our sacred duty," Zui said.

Ayzili snorted. "They've filled his ears with sand." She ruffled his hair affectionately. The young monk smiled, thrilled at the attention she was giving him. His cheeks flushed red as he walked up to the doors barring their path. A series of locks and gears crisscrossed the iron plating here. Zui began to rearrange them in a set pattern. Carlos tried to memorize the combination of switches and dials but soon lost count. Instead he focused on the elaborate carvings that decorated the hall. One looked familiar, a checked heart with a dagger piercing its side.

"This same pattern is woven into the silk of your tent, er tapo," he said to Ayzili. "That's your guardian lwa, your met tet?" The monk and Ayzili exchanged glances. This was clearly a fact any child here would know.

"Yes, that's the sign of my lwa," she said and then turned her attention back to the door. After much tinkering, a clicking noise erupted from the mechanism, and the gears swung into motion. It reminded Carlos of the mechanics behind a clock face, as lock after lock sprung loose. Once the final bolt had pulled free, the doors groaned and inched open a few feet.

Carlos was not prepared for what he saw next. Bathed in pale moonlight, the courtyard that lay before them was so vast, they couldn't even see its walls. Wind rustled through clusters of palm fronds overhead, carrying with it the scent of Hibiscus and Jasmine. These palms bordered an array of winding paths that led off in countless directions. The main trail swept past an impressive monument, three statues of men in kingly robes, who gazed forward as if guarding the entrance. Looking past their stone crowns, Carlos could see a few stars dotting the evening sky.

"A little Garden of Eden," Henry said. Zui looked taken aback as if he'd committed blasphemy.

"Of Simbi. The Garden of Simbi," he corrected. To Carlo's surprise Henry leaned close to Ayzili.

"And who's Simbi?" he asked her.

"Lwa of fresh water and magic." As if to highlight her words, the doors closed behind them with a reverberated echo.

"Did you say magic?" Henry asked, a thoughtful tone overtaking his voice. He strolled to the foot of one of the three statues and laid a hand on the lichen there. Fireflies danced about the stonework overhead.

"Yes, I did." Ayzili sounded impatient to keep moving.

Henry clasped his hands back together. Then he began to twirl his ring. "The word Magic comes from 'magi', as in the three wise men." He gestured to the three statues. Then he bent low to inspect a carving at their base.

"I hear water...is there a spring here?" Carlos asked, trying to allay the suspicious looks Zui was giving them. He knew that Henry was only distracting himself with theology, something he often did. But they were regarded as strange enough already. Random musings weren't going to dispel that. And right now, they needed to instill confidence. Without this trust, they stood no chance of investigating the girl's murder.

"Yes, the only source." Ayzili said. "This is the heart of Ginen."

"How does water reach the rest of the city?"

"Through pipes." She stamped her foot on the grass to indicate that they were underground. Ayzili then led them along a stone path that ran abreast a stream. Moss covered its banks and made the trail slick at times. Eventually it widened into a grove of mango trees. "The orchard," she said as they past through the rows. "The crop is good this season."

A row of boulders enclosed the orchard. Ducking through a notch, they were greeted with a blast of mist and sound - a waterfall. The water cascaded over a ledge and fell twenty feet into a dark basin. Thick tropical plants grew at the pool's edge: hibiscus and palmettos. The whole scene had a strange, calming effect, like a photograph from a Hawaiian travel brochure.

"This is incredible," Henry said, brushing aside a bougainvillea vine. He seemed much calmer now that he was back in a theological mindset. Kneeling before the pool, he cupped his palm full of water.

"Hmm. It fizzes. Taste it." Carlos followed suit. Indeed, the water had a sparkling, copper-rich taste to it.

"Wash your wound," Ayzili said. She dipped a hollow Calabash gourd into the basin and beckoned Carlos towards her. Then she gently unbuttoned his shirt and emptied the contents of the gourd over his cut. The wound burned fiercely, then went cool.

Next, Ayzili pulled her own shirt loosely over one shoulder, exposing a breast. Zui averted his gaze, embarrassed. But Ayzili didn't care. She poured the water over the scrapes on her shoulder and then covered up again.

Carlos let out a long sigh. Finally, he felt safe. These gardens had a calming influence he couldn't explain. Water bubbled at his toes. Cool breezes stirred the air. A firefly came to rest on his knee.

A lightning bug in the desert. It fit somehow. Carlos decided it was time to start asking about the murder.

"Hungar accused us of being involved with that girl's death."

"He's just trying to protect his hide," Ayzili said. "Finish your bath."

"If we're being accused, I'd like to see the evidence."

"You must stay in the gardens tonight," Zui said, scraping two stones over a staff on the beach. "The high priesthood gave strict orders." Sparks flew from the stones, igniting the oil within.

"Can we meet the high priesthood tonight?" Carlos asked.

"No, not until the morning," Zui said.

"How about the council?"

Zui shook his head. "They're not in session."

"Well then, can I at least see the crime scene?" Most of his old cases had been solved within several days or not at all. It was vital they start immediately.

Ayzili turned away from the falls and stared into his eyes long and hard. "You need to stay here and rest your minds. There's a guest room in the hermitage at the far end of the garden. Zui will show you."

"Our heads are fine," Carlos said. "The baka didn't affect us."

"Ours were messed up to begin with —" Henry added, before Carlos cut him short with an elbow.

"Are the baka's venemous?" he asked.

"No, but those who survive an attack often suffer nightmares, confusion." She pointed to her head. "You may not realize it, but you've gone numb with shock. Your speech is off."

"Our speech is different, because we're not from Ginen," Carlos said evenly. "And I have special skills to track that creature. Please, take me to the girl's house, before the trail goes cold."

"Ayzili, no." Zui looked horrified that she would even consider letting them out of the garden.

"What harm can it do?" Carlos asked. He saw the fire dance in Ayzili's eyes as she considered it. The thought of defying the high priests' orders seemed to have won her over.

"All right," she said at last.

Chapter 10

They left Zui at the garden doors as he disapproved of their returning to the city and refused to join them on their field trip. It had already taken Ayzili several minutes just to convince him to unlock the garden's doors.

After traveling through several stately corridors and chambers, they emerged from the inner sanctums of the city into the familiar maze of alleys and flats. As it was now late in the evening, the marketplace had emptied out, and a slight mist hung in the air beneath the canopies. Ayzili held a torch to light their path.

"Her father's out on expedition. So friends will bury her," she said, ducking between two booths. "They'll be here all night."

Apparently the little girl had lots of friends, for the wake was quite crowded. The courtyard in front of them brimmed with tables, each displaying bowls of chicken, jugs of wine, and rolled up snacks Carlos couldn't identify. People walked amongst the food without touching a morsel, some visibly sobbing, others smiling as they told stories.

"What expedition was her father with?" Carlos asked as they followed Ayzili into the crowd.

"One along the coast. To collect yamala." She must have read the confusion on his face for she motioned to the dagger sheathed at her ankle. "Poison. It's how we kill the baka. You don't know this?"

"Got it. I'm a quick learner," Carlos said. "So she was home alone?"

"Yes, very unwise." Ayzili shook head. "But a neighbor checked on her before she went to bed and then found her the next afternoon." They sidestepped a crackling fire pit, in which a heap of rag dolls burnt. Before Carlos could comment on this, an old man grabbed Ayzili's wrist.

"Do you have any hoholi?" he asked.

"No, you don't need that," she shook off his grip and moved toward the front door.

"What'd he want?" Henry asked.

"To throw seeds into the coffin. Distracts the bocors." Realizing they still didn't understand, she added, "Protects the dead from evil priests."

"You're talking about zombies?" Henry joked. Ayzili's stare wiped the smile from his face. She shook her head and then pushed them under a purple curtain draped across the doorway.

Beneath the fabric was a thick wooden door, currently open. Carlos figured the girl would've secured this if she were home alone. Ayzili confirmed it; the neighbor said the door was locked the previous evening and found open when he returned in the morning. So Carlos checked for signs of forced entry. He found none.

"Is this the only entrance?"

"Yes, except for a window inside, but it's barred."

So the girl opened the door herself, or else someone had a key, Carlos thought. Both options pointed to someone close to the victim. Ayzili didn't know how many keys existed, however, or who had them.

"Can I speak to this neighbor?" he asked.

"Yes, later."

"The sooner the better." Carlos turned his attention to the rest of the home and tried to commit it to memory. At his age, that wasn't a good idea. He wished he had his old sketchpad.

The inside of the house flickered gold from dozens of lamps. Little more than wicks floating in bowls of oil, the lights were scattered about the home's monastic furniture – on shelves, tables, chairs, and a family altar lined with clay pots. A pungent citrus smell lingered in the air, masking the odors of food outside. Carlos shivered. His daughter's favorite perfume had that same lemon-lime fragrance. Memories of it ran screaming through his head.

He did a quick walkthrough of the house until he found the smell's origin: a stone tub in an adjoining bathroom. A woman crouched over it with bucket at hand. She dipped a sponge into the water and squeezed out the excess before dabbing, what Carlos realized, was the forehead of the dead girl propped up in the tub. The stench of decay reached out through the sweet perfume and stung their nostrils.

Henry made the sign of the cross and then laid a hand on his friend's shoulder. "Are you all right?"

Carlos nodded. Although he didn't see any visions of his daughter, he could feel her presence. In some form, she was here in this room. The emotion was hard to shake. But he had a job to do. He took a deep breath and examined the body.

The deceased bore the signs of an elaborate ceremony. Cotton had been placed in her ears and nostrils and the sign of a cross drawn above her eyes in flour. A strip of satin looped under her chin and over her head, as if to prevent her jaw from opening.

"Who's she talking to?" Henry asked, noticing that the woman was whispering into the dead girl's ear.

Ayzili bit her lip. "Sasha. But her soul's not there. The baka has it."

A knot formed in Carlos's stomach as he examined the injuries. Jagged cuts ripped across her neck and stomach; they were consistent with an animal mauling and would've lead to massive blood loss, the likely cause of death. There were also lacerations and bruises on her forearms - defensive wounds. She had tried to fight off her attacker. He clenched his jaw and then tilted his head to observe her back.

It showed signs of fixed lividity, shoulder blades stained purple where the blood had pooled. She'd been dead at least 6-8 hours.

"May I see her hands?" he asked the woman with the sponge. She nodded and, struggling against the rigor mortis, lifted the dead girl's wrist. "Did you clean these? Was there any blood beneath her nails?" The woman shook her head, no. "Thank you." Carlos turned back to Ayzili.

"Where was she found?"

"In her room. Back there."

Sasha's room resembled more a prison cell than somewhere a child might sleep. An empty table was all that decorated the barren room. Carlos noted the bars on the window, just as Ayzili had said.

"Why so empty?" he asked, bending close to the ground. It had obviously been cleaned, blood spatter scrubbed from the tiles with a fresh layer of sand tossed over them. He noticed a few breadcrumbs amongst the grains.

Ayzili sighed as if she were explaining the obvious. "They've burnt her belongings."

"Wouldn't her father want something to remember her by?"

"And risk being haunted?" Ayzili crossed her arms. "Why are you asking so many questions?"

Carlos stood and wiped the sand from his hands. "I used to do this for a living, you know."

"You made a living from death?"

"No, from catching those who cause it." He scanned the room carefully. On the ceiling were flecks of high-velocity impact spatter but not enough to determine an area of origin. If only he'd been here earlier. This scene was too contaminated now to be of much use.

"Did they find the key to the house?"

"Yes," Ayzili said, "it was in the girl's hand."

"Any blood on it?"

Ayzili put her hands to her hips. "I don't know."

"Can you find out?" This was vital. It could tell him if the victim had the key when she was killed, or if someone planted it post-mortem. Either she had unlocked the door, or a perp had staged things to make it look that way. Carlos was about to explain all this when something caught his eye in the corner of the room. "Get rid of that torch."

"What?" Ayzili stared at him as if he were crazy.

"Hard to find clues in the dark, Carlo," said Henry.

"No, sometimes it's easier." Carlos kept his eyes locked on the far corner. As Ayzili took the flame outside and the room darkened, a tiny smudge on the floor began to glow. He crouched over the tile in question.

"What's that?" Henry asked.

"Trace evidence. You know what it looks like...when our people worked a crime scene they'd spray this chemical Luminol. It reacts to the iron in blood, 'causes latent stains to glow."

Henry peered closer at the splotch. "But they can't have access to that stuff here?"

"No. I think it's something else." Carlos scratched his chin and stared at the wall. He could hear Ayzili speaking with someone in the adjacent room.

"Can't send it to the lab here," Henry said. "So what's your guess?"

"Are you boys done?" Ayzili returned with the torch. From her tone, Carlos got the sense she was humoring them. She pitied their fate. The baka had destroyed their minds, after all. They were babbling nonsense. Well, he had to show her differently.

Carlos rose and faced Ayzili. "The gardens. Access to them's controlled, right?"

"Yes," she said. "Only a high priest, a guest under their escort, or a member of the council may enter."

"Did the vic...did Sasha visit the gardens recently?"

"I don't think so."

"How about the priest who was performing her death rites?" Carlos asked.

Ayzili shook her head. "He was from this quarter. Not a high priest."

"How about any of her friends? Did any council members come by? "

"Not likely. Very few visit the gardens."

"But you and that young monk, Zui, both did." He pointed at her. "Have either of you been in this room before now?"

"No, why does this matter?" Her eyebrow arched in suspicion.

Carlos crouched down again, swabbed at the glowing streak with his index finger, and rubbed it against his thumb. "Cause of this trace residue."

"Residue from what?" Henry asked.

"A firefly." As soon as he said this, Ayzili's expression changed to one of concern.

"Fireflies only live in the garden," she said.

Carlos smiled. "Locard's exchange principle - every contact leaves a trace."

"Which means?" Henry asked.

"The killers came from the gardens. It's our secondary crime scene."

Ayzili shook her head. "A baka couldn't open the garden doors —"

"But a person can," Carlos said. "Look, this residue is almost faded. Fireflies appear in the evening. Whatever tracked it in, they were here around the time of death."

"You're suggesting the creature had help?" Henry shuddered even as he said it.

Carlos stood up. "I bet someone led the creature here, unlocked the door, then once Sasha was killed, planted the key on her body to throw us off track." He paused for emphasis. "And I think they came from the gardens." Mambo's words about greedy men rang in his ears. What would motivate someone to put a child's life in jeopardy? He couldn't fathom it.

Maybe the answer was simpler. The girl had inexplicably opened the door in the middle of the night. The baka happened to be nearby and saw its chance - a crime of opportunity. Carlos shook his head. It didn't feel right. The baka had assistance. His gut told him this went deep.

"We need to find out who was in the gardens recently, who might have access to the key, and who knew Sasha would be home alone. That's our list of suspects." He looked to Ayzili, hoping he'd made an impression. She chewed her lip for a moment, digesting everything he'd said.

"Tomorrow we can ask Zui," she said at last. "He's probably still upset I took you outside the gardens. Come, we'll talk to that neighbor now."

"You trust me then?" Carlos asked. He searched her face for signs of acknowledgment.

Ayzili thought long and hard before replying. "The key they found in Sasha's hand...," she said slowly, "...it was the only thing not covered in blood."

Chapter 11

A portly man opened the door with a scowl beneath his woolly beard. Carlos and Henry instinctively took a step backwards. The man had tattoos running up the length of his arms and looked like he'd be quite comfortable in a Daytona Biker Bar. His girth took up most of the doorway.

But it was his face that seemed so familiar to Carlos, and at once he remembered where he'd seen him before. This man had performed the young girl's death rites. He was a priest. Out of his clerical robes, Carlos barely recognized him. But Ayzili certainly did. She broke into a weak smile and embraced the man like a long lost sister.

"I was hoping you'd come by." He matched Ayzili's smile with one of his own.

"These are the men I told you about."

"Please come in." The big man sighed. "I'm sorry for not greeting you at the marketplace. The body wasn't yet safe." He stepped aside and motioned for the three to enter into the candlelit interior.

The décor was not what Carlos had expected. Parchment covered a table in the center of the room, and crumbling bookshelves lined its walls like some medieval library. Three children stared up at them from the table, pausing midway through their writing.

"Go on to bed, little ones," the man said and collected their papers. Then he turned to his guests. "I'm sorry for the mess." He scraped a crust of candle wax from the table. "We were conducting a late lesson. I'm Jelosquevo, but please call me —"

"Jellyman," Ayzili said, still smiling.

"Jell is fine. I run this orphanage."

"Why are you..." Henry's voice trailed off when he noticed several glass vases around the room filled with water. Inside each pulsed a glowing jellyfish. Their light seemed to illuminate the room. "Oh..." he said at last.

Ayzili introduced Carlos and Henry to the Jellyman. She quickly brought him up to speed, explaining their visit to the crime scene and what Carlos had discovered there. The tone in her voice betrayed some lingering skepticism. As Jell listened, his features hardened.

"Give me a chance," Carlos said. "I want to help." What he didn't want was to be treated like a child. He suspected that was the real reason Ayzili had brought them here. She still considered them mental cases. And Jell took care of Ginen's lost causes, the young and abandoned.

"Jell was the last to see Sasha alive," Ayzili said. "He's the neighbor I told you about."

"So the door was locked when you left?" Carlos asked.

"I made sure of that. Promised her father I would check on her every night."

Carlos knew he had to tread carefully here. "Do you have a key?" he asked.

The large priest leaned forward in his chair, fully aware of what that question implied. His weight caused the chair to creak menacingly. "As I told Hungar, there are only two keys. Sasha had one, her father has the other."

"I'm not accusing you of anything," Carlos said.

Jell nodded. "I understand. You're just seeking the truth." He rubbed the sleep from his eyes. "I heard reports that she'd missed her studies. So this afternoon I went to check on her." He ran his large hands over his face, wincing as he relived what he'd seen. "I found her in her room."

Carlos asked a few more questions. When it became clear that the priest was tiring, he thanked him, suggesting they continue in the morning.

Jell sat back in his chair. "I can't imagine anyone spending the night with those fools up in the Gardens. You're welcome to stay here, but the school's crowded tonight as I've given roof to several kids off the street. However, you can sleep in the peristyle." He sighed. "Sasha's mass isn't until morning."

"The peri-what?" Henry asked. He'd been pacing through the room with interest. Several portraits on the wall had caught his eye, all of them Catholic saints.

"Jell is Hougen for this quarter's peristyle," Ayzili explained as if she were lecturing a child.

Henry paused in front of an icon depicting St. Peter. "How long have you been a priest?" he asked.

"I'm more of a teacher."

Henry gestured to another of the portraits. "That explains Catherine of Alexandria, patron saint of libraries and students."

"You're canzo?" The Jellyman's face registered shock, and then he laughed. "No wonder she called your minds' sick. She's not fond of spiritual men."

Ayzili eyed Henry suspiciously. "Had I known, I might have left him by the baka hole where I found him." She crossed her arms.

"Saint Catherine's known for debating theology," Henry started. But Carlos shot him a look that told him to stop right there. So Henry took a seat.

Jell slapped him on the back. "That's indeed the lwa of libraries. But we call her by a different name."

"What is that?"

Ayzili rolled her eyes. "Our time's better spent —"

"Don't mind her," Jell interrupted. "She seeks a different path."

"Jell, this is not the time." Ayzili put her hands to her hips – it was obvious she'd heard this conversation before and was not going to hear it again.

"I'm sorry." Jell quickly sobered. Carlos hid a smile. He and Henry had played out this conversation whenever he'd skipped church to go fishing. To break the awkward silence, Jell offered them a loaf of crusty bread and some olives.

"What are you writing?" Henry asked between mouthfuls, eyeing the thick leather tomb open faced on the table.

"A history of Ginen."

"No kidding," Henry remarked. "A historian. I do a little of that as well."

Carlos caught his friend's eye. He couldn't believe their good luck. If anyone could provide them answers about this strange world, it was a scholar. A priest and a historian - the similarities between Henry and the Jellyman were mounting up eerily. Carlos knew his friend would soon bond with this local priest. Henry's religious misgivings had never been a match for his curiosity.

"Where do you do your research?" Henry asked.

"The archives. I've asked the high priests for permission to enter, but they're too holy for the likes of me. So, I've got an inside source." A smile crept across his face. "Want to see what I've found?" Jell walked over to a shelf and thumbed through several rolls of parchment. Selecting one, he ambled back to the table and unrolled the paper in front of the others, weighing down its corners with candles.

"This is the most complete map I've ever seen...shows all the outlying territories." He waved his hand across the paper. The map was extremely detailed, the surface inked in narrow lines. However, it contained vast blank spaces, which Carlos guessed were stretches of desert. The coastline stretched down one side, curving to the far edges of the paper.

"That's the ocean?" Carlos asked.

"Yes, home of the lwa." Jell's hand drifted over the water to a small circle on the beach. "Here we are in Ginen," he said, tapping his finger.

"What's the scale?" Carlos asked. When Jell didn't respond he rephrased, "How many miles per inch?"

"From here to here would take a day's walk." His finger barely moved across the paper, revealing the immense scope of the map.

"There were four other cities, now destroyed by the baka." He pointed them out across the desert. "Which are you from?"

"None of them," Carlos said. "We came from somewhere else."

Ayzili cleared her throat as if to say, 'I told you these men were still in shock.'

Carlos didn't want to dwell on his mental state. "How old are your cities?" he asked.

"We don't know," Jell said. "We didn't build them."

Henry leaned forward, his curiosity piqued. "Then who did?"

"Those who came before us. Would you care for a drink?" Without waiting for an answer, Jell got up and retrieved several mugs from the next room. Then he uncorked a bottle and poured out a dark liquid. "Cider from the gardens," he said, bringing the mug up to his nostrils. "Also smuggled out by my source."

"So who came before you? And where did your people come from?"

"Those are the answers I seek," Jell said. "All I've found are legends thus far." He leaned back again and took a swig of cider. Carlos had the feeling Jell had told this story many times to the children of his orphanage.

"The old ones say Ginen has existed forever, from the beginning of time. But not always in peace. Every few centuries the baka grow in strength and number. They storm the cities and kill many people." Jell squeezed his fist and then slowly opened it.

"The survivors, so shocked by this massacre, forget their past. As time goes on, they slowly rebuild. Ginen flourishes again. And the circle repeats itself, as it always has." He set his mug down and locked eyes with his guests. "That's what the legends say."

"Why do the baka kill?" Carlos asked.

"They're animals," Ayzili said. Her smile was gone, fingers tracing the rim of her mug. "Why do we kill chickens? Because we like the taste of their meat." Coldness permeated her voice.

"Possibly." Jell shrugged. "But others say the baka grow stronger due to the greed of men. Their weakness gives the creatures strength."

This sounded familiar. "What do these men get in return?" Carlos asked.

"Precious stones that the baka mine deep beneath the sands."

This fit with Mambo's theory that greedy men were behind the baka's rise to power. But Carlos knew the danger of focusing too intently on one theory; you become blind to other possibilities. "How else would anyone profit from Sasha's death?" he asked.

Ayzili shook her head. She seemed relieved he was focusing on the facts again. "They wouldn't. They're just random victims."

"Victims?" Carlos noticed she had used the plural.

Ayzili bit her lip. "There have been many killings inside Ginen this year. The baka bleed us from within."

"Where were the others killed?"

Jell unfolded another map, a layout of the city's streets and alleys. Then he pointed out the homes where these deaths occurred. Balling up globs of wax, Carlos marked each crime scene. They were scattered throughout the city in no discernible pattern, at least no obvious one.

Carlos had faced similar situations running serial task forces out of Miami Dade. The last one involved a string of prostitute deaths, all strangled in the same manner. He'd pored over the case files, searching the crime scene photos for a common denominator. The answer had been staring him in the face the whole time - orange traffic cones. One was present at each scene, for the killer had worked roadside construction, selecting his victims while on the job, then returning after hours to take their lives.

So what's the common denominator here? The murders were spread about the city, the victims varying ages and genders. It seemed random. With no case files to flip through, he'd have to conduct interviews. But he doubted the locals would open up to a stranger. He'd definitely need Jell's help, a man trusted in the community. Regardless, it would all have to wait for tomorrow. Carlos yawned.

"Let me get some bedding," Jell said. After he had gathered three blankets, he led them through a side hallway. The corridor emptied into a wide courtyard scattered with lemon and mapou trees. Ribbons, tied to their branches, flapped gently in the night breeze.

"Nice school," Carlos said, surveying the perimeter. Classrooms flanked either side, wooden benches stacked up for the night.

Jell led the way, his feet treading the packed earthen floor. "Watch out for the reposoirs," he said.

"What are those?" Henry asked.

Jell pointed to a cement collar that ringed one of the trees. Then he put a finger to his lips. "The children are sleeping,"

Carlos followed his gaze through a dormitory window, where he caught a glimpse of hammocks. They were lined up in rows like berths in a ship, each cradling a sleeping child.

So many orphans.

Carlos wondered what fate their parents had endured? His gut told him he already knew the answer to that. If it weren't for Ayzili, he would've shared the same end.

At the back of the courtyard, they came upon a tall, open-air pavilion. Benches surrounded the space, encircling a central pole that extended to the roof.

"There's plenty of room for all of you here," Jell said. "Sasha's coffin won't arrive until dawn."

"What is this place?" Henry asked, his eyes wide and suspicious. He noticed drums suspended from the rafters.

Jell gestured about the pavilion. "My Peristyle, where we honor the lwa."

Henry shivered, obviously not too keen on spending the night in a voodoo temple. His attention came to rest on the floor. Charcoal patterns decorated the ground here, encircling the central pole. Jell caught his eye and rested a hand against the column.

"The gateway between the Lwa Sea below and the land of men..." He pointed to the floor patterns. "The veves call the spirits up to us."

"These designs are called veves?" Carlos asked, crouching closer to inspect one.

"Yes, they help us call a specific lwa," Jell said, his demeanor changed to that of a storyteller. Clearly, he enjoyed teaching. Crossing over a design that resembled a crop field, Jell regarded his guest as if they were students.

"This one's Azaka, spirit of farmers."

"Well, the patron saint of farmers is Saint Isidore," Henry said.

Jell shrugged and moved to the next symbol. "This one's Ogoun, spirit of warriors and metalworkers."

"Saint Jacques?" Henry asked, but Jell didn't recognize this name either. The design looked nothing like war, a triangle with a line and some swirls.

"And this one..." Jell paused over the image of a checkered heart. "Ayzili can tell you about this one...although she's never been taken by a spirit."

The smile vanished from Henry's face. "What do you mean taken?" His brow cinched in disapproval.

"Goodnight Jell," Ayzili said, escorting him back to the courtyard. "We'll leave before the funeral procession."

He nodded reluctantly and then followed her back into the trees to have a word in private. This left Carlos and Henry alone for a moment.

Carlos used the opportunity to explain his interview strategy for the following day. He'd take Jell and talk to anyone who knew the victim. Then they'd find Zui and snoop around the gardens some more - follow up on the firefly lead.

Henry scratched his beard and sat down on one of the benches. "You really think your cop stuff will work here?"

"It's worth a shot. Solving the murders will get us in their good graces," Carlos said. "They might even help us fight our way back home."

Henry nodded. He couldn't argue with that logic. "So where do you think we are? The Bermuda triangle?"

"I don't know."

"I'll bet you anything the answer's in the archives," Henry said.

Carlos knew his friend couldn't resist the lure of a library, even one he considered sacrilegious. He noticed that Henry had already begun to rotate his seminary ring.

"Yes, we need to get in there." Henry seemed embarrassed by his enthusiasm and changed the subject. "Spirit Possession, huh? I thought Jell might be on the level until I heard that." He walked around the temple, eyeing a bundle of roots and ship model dangling from the rafters. "So, this is where Mambo sacrifices her virgins?" He tried on a straw hat that hung from the wall.

"Usually just rum and candles. Sometimes chicken. Here you go..." Carlos spotted a plate of fried pork behind the column.

"How do you know all this?" Henry asked.

"Near the end, Naomi built one of these altars in our apartment. Her family's from Haiti, you know."

"Everyone deals with loss in their own way," Henry said, inspecting the fried meat. "I just wish she'd embraced —"

"Food shouldn't be wasted on the dead." Ayzili reentered the pavilion. She had a habit of sneaking up on people, Carlos noted. He watched as she strode across the temple and snatched up a few pieces of pork. Gulping them down, she cast a disapproving look at Henry's new hat. Then she reached for her blanket.

"I'm going to sleep," she said. "We meet with the council early tomorrow." So much for my interview plans, Carlos thought. They'll have to wait, I guess.

Soon the three had arranged their bedding around the center pillar and laid down to rest. Snores immediately drifted up to the ceiling, where a solitary figure had just slipped through a window and onto one of the rafters. A dagger gleamed in the moonlight, clenched tightly in his free hand.

Chapter 12

This night it was Henry who couldn't sleep. He rolled onto his stomach just as a shadow passed unnoticed in the rafters overhead. Staring into the charcoal symbols covering the floor, he felt a growing tide of worry rise in his chest. *Where the hell am I?* He'd never paid Mambo's superstitions much heed. She was stuck in her ways, and no amount of lecturing on his part was going to change that. But now he was immersed in her world, and that terrified him more than anything. *If this isn't a test of faith, what is it?*

Only one thing kept him calm: the glimpses of Christianity he saw everywhere. Bits of familiarity, he could hold onto these puzzle pieces and find comfort there. *Instead of spirits...they are just patron saints. And the floor patterns - religious icons.* That he could understand. He began tracing one of the designs with his finger, when a thought occurred to him.

"Carlos, you asleep?" he asked.

"I was."

"I just realized something about this icon here..."

Carlos groaned. "Can't it wait until tomorrow?"

"It's the same as the medallion Mambo gave you."

"We'll ask Jell about it in the morning," Carlos groaned. "I saw roosters out there. Let's get some sleep while we can —"

A pair of dirty boots slammed into the dust. Startled, Carlos and Henry looked up. That's all they could do before the man reached back with his dagger. Then a metal dish slammed into his face. The force knocked loose a spray of saliva and sent him crashing hard to the floor. Carlos and Henry scrambled out of his reach.

The assassin cursed and used his burlap vest to wipe the blood from his lip. A plate, which Ayzili had just thrown, lay rattling at his feet. She stood before him, one hand clutching a sword. This weapon was more than a match for his rusted dagger. And she knew it too. Her eyes blinked back calm and unafraid.

But the assassin had one card left to play, for his dagger gleamed with a thin coat of poison. He gripped its hilt and spun the knife violently towards his foe. With one elegant move, Ayzili swung upwards with her blade. The assassin's knife clattered harmlessly across the dirt. Utterly defenseless, he stared into her eyes. No pity or remorse shown in those red irises. She ran at him. Her sword sliced down fiercely. The assassin winced, but the sharp edge had come to a halt inches from his nose. Carlos had thrust his buck knife against the blade.

"We need him to talk."

"He'll only tell you lies." She leaned in and pressed harder.

"For the love of God," Henry tried to pull Ayzili back, but she shook him off.

Carlos held firm. "I can't let you kill him."

Ayzili turned her head in his direction, her green eyes bloodshot and piercing. Then her expression softened, and she retracted the sword.

"Only because it's you."

Carlos cast her a wary glance and then moved his knife towards the assassin's throat. He pulled him to a standing position. "Easy," he said. "Answer carefully and you'll live." The man was sweating profusely and shaking. Carlos knew it wasn't because of him.

"Dante, have mercy," the assassin pleaded. "Forgive me." Ayzili ignored his strange words, her attention rapt on Carlos's next move.

"Why were you trying to kill us?" Carlos asked. The man's eyes darted to Ayzili as if gauging whether or not he should respond. He exhaled nervously, his breath stinking of onions and kerosene.

"I had to," he cried out. "You know of the garden."

Carlos lowered his voice. "I can protect you, as long as you cooperate." He marveled to himself how Ayzili had fallen into step with the good cop, bad cop routine. Carlos had usually played the angry cop back in Miami. But something was wrong here. Ayzili played her part too well. Carlos sensed she really would kill this man in cold blood. It was not for show.

"Did you lead the baka to that girl?" he asked. "To Sasha's home?"

The man murmured pitifully. "I had no choice." The quick confession startled Carlos. He must really fear Ayzili.

A shout echoed across the courtyard. Their fight had evidentially awoken the school. Using this distraction, the assassin made a break for it. But he had gone no more than a few feet, when he staggered forward as if struck by something, collapsing to the ground with a thud. A knife hilt protruded from his shoulder blades. It was his weapon; the poison had worked fast.

"Damn it." Carlos glanced at Ayzili but she shook her head as if to say, it wasn't me. He heard footsteps and glanced up to see Hungar approaching with Jell and a row of guards. "Son of a bitch," Carlos cursed. "That was our only link. Why'd you kill him?"

"We did not," Hungar said, his eyes blazing. "What happened here?"

Henry tried to diffuse the situation. "This man here tried to kill us," he said. "Then someone threw a knife at him from the shadows...over there." He gestured across the courtyard.

Hungar nodded to his men to fan out and secure the school. Then he bent low to take the assassin's pulse. Finding, none he rose to meet Ayzili.

"I told you they were to stay in the gardens," he said coldly. "This blood's on your hands." Ayzili brushed the hair from her eyes and returned the stare. She seemed oddly out of breath.

"Convenient timing. You tailing us?" she asked, launching into an angry tirade. By now a small crowd of children and teachers had gathered. Jell ordered them to move away from the scene, instructing the teachers to set up a perimeter barricade. Turning away from the chaos, Carlos bent over the body of the assassin. He had to inspect the crime scene while it was still fresh. The man's face rang familiar...but from where? "I've seen you before," he whispered.

"Are you sure he's dead?" Henry asked from some distance away. He was used to death, but the kind cleaned up and lying in a casket. From his shaking hands, it was obvious the violence had rattled him. Carlos put a finger to the man's neck.

"Yeah. He's gone."

Henry leaned in closer, nodding. "The light's gone out of his eyes."

"Yeah...wait, what did you say?"

The light's gone out.

Ayzili and Hungar, meanwhile, had almost come to blows. "I'm warning you," Hungar shouted. "I'll put you outside the gates tonight." Carlos stepped in between them.

"That man on the floor," he asked, "what does he do for a living?"

Hungar swore and then squinted at the corpse. "He's a lamplighter."

Carlos snapped his fingers. "It's the traffic cone. I knew it."

"What do you know?" Ayzili asked.

"How the baka is getting through the city unnoticed."

"And how would you know that?" Hungar asked.

"Because we passed this man last night when he was lighting torches."

"So?" Hungar had lost all patience, and Carlos knew he'd better make his point quickly.

"So what better hiding place...than a giant cart?"

* * *

Hungar wasn't impressed with his theory about the lamplighter's cart. Even when Carlos explained how most of the murders had occurred near main streets – addresses the lamplighter would have cause to visit – the large Captain just shook his head, hardly listening.

He told them that the high priesthood had ordered their return to the gardens, and he'd come to enforce the ruling. Ayzili countered that the council had ordered the men released into her custody, not the high priesthood's. Where they spent the night was irrelevant. But she relented so as not to cause a scene at the school.

"Since when do you enforce the rule of the high priesthood over the council?" she asked as they marched into the street.

"I can't afford to make enemies of either," Hungar said.

Ayzili snorted. "Your job's not to make people happy, it's to make them safe."

Outside the orphanage, they were greeted with a stark sight - the lamplighter's cart, abandoned by the side of the road. A cloth, draping its sides, flapped gently in the morning breezes. Otherwise, it was deadly calm. Before they could move past it, the wind blew hard against the fabric, pressing it briefly against an unmistakable form beneath the wheels. They all recognized its shape – the sharp angles of a claw. Everyone drew a weapon except Carlos and Henry. The guards froze in their tracks and looked to Hungar for a signal to attack.

Ayzili didn't have the patience.

She marched right up to the cart and yanked back the cloth. The crouched form of a giant crab stared back at her, its legs tucked beneath itself. The creature took up most of the space beneath the cart and looked coiled to strike.

"Ayzili, watch out," Carlos yelled, but she didn't flinch. Instead, she reached under the cart and grabbed a hold of the shell. With one great tug, she pulled the crab out from beneath the wheels and let it collapse into the dust with a crunch.

"It's just a shedding," she said. "The baka's elsewhere." Peering closer, Carlos saw what she meant. What he'd thought was a live crab had only been the remains of its molting, perfectly formed in the hollow dimensions of the creature. Tattoos covered its carapace, with one in particular glistening fresh in the pale dawn light. Ayzili pointed to the mark and cursed.

"That's Sasha's met tet. It killed her."

"The baka shed their skin? Carlos asked. "Is it fresh?"

"No," Hungar kicked the shell. "It's old." He glowered at Ayzili. "If you hadn't killed the lamplighter, we might've known where it's hiding."

"Look. It wasn't me," Ayzili said. "Someone killed him from the shadows. Are you going to stand here arguing all morning, or are you going to find that demon?"

Hungar was about to snap back, but he thought better of it and held his tongue. Then he turned to his men. "Let's check out his home. Do any of you know its location?"

One of the guards answered affirmatively, and Hungar gestured for him to lead the way down the street. Ayzili didn't follow.

"They'll never find it," she said as Hungar disappeared around the corner. Before she could elaborate, they heard footsteps behind them. A large parade was marching their way. In the center of this throng, two men supported a tiny coffin on their heads.

Ayzili lowered her eyes. "It's Sasha."

The funeral procession was unlike any Carlos had ever seen. The pallbearers wove back and forth erratically, sometimes spinning around completely.

"Are they drunk?" Henry asked.

Ayzili shook her head. "They're confusing the spirit, so she won't find her way back and torment the living." She dragged the crab skin behind the cart to hide it from view. The procession marched past them without so much as a glance and disappeared into the school. Ayzili sighed. "They needn't worry. The baka has her spirit now."

Chapter 13

The Jellyman provided them with a breakfast of sweet tasting bread that Carlos and Henry devoured hungrily. Ayzili didn't touch the food. Instead, she took swigs from a flask concealed beneath the table. With each drink, she locked eyes with Henry as if daring him to say something. Carlos had sensed a rift between the two ever since Ayzili had learned Henry was a priest.

"Do you mind?" Henry asked, reaching for her flask. To Ayzili's surprise, he took a long swig and then wiped his beard clean. "Thanks," he said, returning to the book on the spirits he'd found.

Jell reappeared from the kitchen and frowned at Ayzili's full plate. "An empty sack can't stand up," he said. "You'll need your strength for the council meeting. Do they know the rules?"

"No, we don't. What rules?" Carlos asked.

"The council is very serious about tradition," Jell said, puffing out his chest in imitation. "Don't speak unless spoken to, always address the group as a whole, never sit before a council member does —"

"Sounds like a fun group," Henry said, licking his thumb to turn a page.

"If you break the rules," Jell said, "you won't be laughing."

"Is this council elected?" Carlos asked, his hands reaching instinctively for a flip pad. "Do you have something I can write with?" His brain could only hold so much information.

After providing him with a quill and paper, Jell explained that Ginen was divided into four quarters, like slices of a giant pie. Residents from each quarter elected representatives to serve on the council. These in turn elected a council head, the de facto president of Ginen.

"His name is Riyal and he's a good man," Jell said. "He enjoys support from most of the people, even though the high priesthood opposes his every move." He went on to explain how the high priesthood had great influence over this, the Northern Quarter, and thus held many seats on the council.

"They should stay in their little monastery and tend grapes," Ayzili said. Carlos agreed that politics and religion shouldn't mix but kept his opinions to himself. The last thing he wanted was to get embroiled in a power struggle.

"We'd better get going," Jell said. "It's almost time."

Flipping his wrist, Carlos remembered that he'd lost his watch for the bribe. He'd have to keep an eye out for that guard.

* * *

Hungar met them deep in the city, by the familiar staircase they had journeyed up the pervious night.

"Ugh. Not again," Henry said.

"Could do you good," Ayzili said, jabbing him in the gut. After a dizzying round of corkscrews and halls, they finally came upon a colossal set of doors that, Carlos guessed, marked the entrance to the council chamber. Hungar nodded to the guards flanking either side, who opened the doors to a blinding light.

The room beyond was round, with windows that overlooked the garden they had visited the other night. Sun rays filled the chamber, and it took a few seconds for Carlo's eyes to adjust.

Lowering his hand, he made out the shapes of several hooded figures. They stood behind desks that bore their names in an elaborate, swirling script. Most wore grey garments, but a select few were dressed in the purple cloth of the high priesthood. Carlos got the immediate impression that some of the council members didn't like him. It was the same look he used to get when he'd drive his cruiser through certain Miami neighborhoods - suspicious stares. An awkward moment of silence passed, and Carlos used the time to glance over his companions. Hungar's face was taught, with beads of sweat dotting his forehead. Carlos sympathized with him. This was a man, after all, charged with knowing everything that went down in the city; yet chaos erupted all around him. Ayzili, in contrast, looked cool and impatient. She returned the stares of each councilman without blinking. At last, an elderly man directly in front of them broke the silence. Although he had the appearance of an octogenarian, his voice was clear and strong.

"Thank you, Ayzili, for bringing these strangers to our attention. They should've been brought here right away." Hungar grimaced but said nothing. The man frowned and then took a seat. With a rustle of movement, everyone else followed suit. This must be Riyal, the head of the council, Carlos figured. The man sure seemed to command authority.

Ayzili tapped her foot anxiously and then blurted out, "At first I thought these men were sick, but they may truly be survivors of the outer territories..." A murmur of disapproval immediately followed her words. She had not been officially addressed. Ayzili rolled her eyes. The old man hid a smile.

"I'd rather hear it from them, Ayzili." His gaze fell upon Carlos. "My name is Riyal, head of this council. What are your names, and where are you from?"

Carlos made a quick introduction and then recounted their story, being as candid as possible. He was just getting to their first encounter with Ayzili, when a tall, skeletal man in a lavender robe interrupted him.

"Your clothes. What are they made of?" His sunken eyes flashed menace as he spoke.

"You mean our —"

"I mean this." He held up Henry's wetsuit. "What is this?"

"It keeps you warm in the ocean," Henry said. "It's called neoprene."

The man's face wrinkled with suspicion. "Why do you enter the ocean? To what end?"

"Surfing," Henry said, clearing his throat. "It's a sport."

"You know what lies in the surf, don't you?" the man asked, moving in for the kill. "Young baka. You're teaching them to infiltrate our city."

"That's nonsense. A sentry attacked them on the dune sea," Ayzili said. "They're not —"

"I wasn't talking to you!" The man's eyes bulged to such a degree, it seemed they might pop from his head. He turned back to Carlos. "How did you know of the shedding beneath the lamplighter's cart?"

"My job, my old job, was as a detective," Carlos said and then, realizing that no one understood him, he added, "I solve crimes."

"Or do you cause them?" Before he could respond, the skeletal man continued, "I don't think you're from some lost island. You're a sorcerer and should be locked away."

Riyal, the council head, raised a hand. "This is not a trial, Sarn."

"If our laws were passed, it would be. I've presented enough evidence."

"But your laws have not passed," Riyal said and then addressed Carlos once more. "Please finish."

Carlos nodded his thanks. "We'd like to head home, but before we go – I believe my skills may be of some use to you."

Riyal considered this for a moment and then said, "Can you tell me why the lamplighter tried to kill you, and who in turn killed him?"

Carlos was beginning to grasp the power dynamics of the council. This was the first thing he always did at any task force meeting back in Miami - figure out who held the ball. Whether it was MDPD, the Sheriff's Office, FDLE, or the FBI, it was vital knowing who wanted the lead and who actually had it. The dynamics of this council weren't terribly different; the same power struggles and shows of bravado were on display here.

Sarn, the head of the high priesthood, was clearly out for blood. He showed no interest in what they had to say, his mind already made up. The chest thumping is all political show, Carlos thought, pure theatre. To Sarn, they were just pawns, useful in promoting an agenda. Riyal, on the other hand, had a cool disposition and was obviously plugged into the happenings on the street. This gave him a lot more credence. Carlos wanted to level with him, although he wished he could do so in private, away from the other council members. Oh, what the hell, he thought.

"I believe the lamplighter tried to kill us...because we were closing in on the truth."

"Explain," Riyal said.

"Last night we visited the home of the slain girl, Sasha. I found evidence from the gardens there."

"He's trying to confuse us," the tall priest named Sarn hissed.

"Let him have his say." Riyal gestured for Carlos to continue.

"I don't know how the gardens fit in, but that knowledge was worth killing us over. That's why they sent an assassin." He paused to collect his thoughts. "Maybe the garden's where the baka enter the city? The lamplighter picks the creatures up there, smuggles them under his cart, and then transports them throughout the city. It's a good cover."

"Convenient that the accused is no longer here to argue these claims," Sarn said.

"Yes. I don't know who killed him," Carlos answered. "It wasn't us."

"None of you witnessed it?" Riyal asked.

Henry raised his hand like a student in class. "I saw the knife fly out of the shadows. But I couldn't tell who threw it."

"Before he died, he mentioned the gardens," Carlos added. "Obviously, someone wanted to silence him."

"You're lying." Sarn jabbed a bony finger into the air. "The lamplighter was prohibited from entering the gardens. He handed his cart over to one of our priests. We would have known if there was a Baka underneath."

"Yes, you would have," Carlos said evenly. It took Sarn a moment to digest what he had said. Then his face turned the color of his robes, and a vein on his forehead began to pulse with rage.

"How dare you? To even suggest our involvement...this is treason!" The man rose to his feet. "I won't listen to this arrogant fool."

"Sit down, Sarn," said Riyal. "There's no need for theatrics."

"I'm not sitting here and taking these insults, Riyal."

"No one's accusing anyone," Carlos said, "but I'd like to speak with the priest responsible for the cart within the garden."

"Who is that?" Ayzili asked. Her eyes scanned the rows of priests. One of her hands clenched into a first.

"Point him out, Sarn," Riyal said sternly. The weight accompanying his tone carried a great deal of authority.

"He's not here. His whereabouts are currently, unknown."

"What's his name?"

"Father Zui," Sarn said thru clenched teeth. Carlos gasped. This was the young monk so enamored with Ayzili, the one who had led them to the gardens. Could he really be involved? Carlos began to doubt his theory. And he wasn't the only one. Sarn continued his mad rant. "Don't tell me you believe this fool? These strangers likely framed the lamplighter to cover their own crimes."

Riyal rose to his feet to address the council as a whole. Immediately, the others fell silent. He paused before speaking, as if gathering his thoughts. "My brother was killed by a baka two weeks ago; now, this girl from the Northern Quarter has died. Attacks are increasing, my friends. The baka grow greedy, and we pay for it in lives."

He took a deep breath of morning air and stared straight ahead at no one. "Captain Hungar, guard these strangers. But allow them full access to the gardens and permission to question Zui. Perhaps they can do what we cannot."

Sarn slammed his fist on the bench before him. He cursed angrily and stormed out of the chamber, brushing roughly against the group as he passed. Other members of the priesthood joined him in exodus.

As Sarn left the chamber, Carlos noticed a glint of metal beneath his sleeve. That bastard has my wristwatch, he thought, and obviously a connection with the city guard. That could spell trouble down the road.

It took several minutes for the council to quiet its ranks. Riyal sighed and massaged his forehead.

"Go," he said at last. "I lay my trust in the hands of strangers. May the lwa guide you in your quest."

* * *

"I'm glad Riyal's on our side," Carlos said, after they'd left the council chambers. "Can we meet with him in person?"

Hunger frowned. "He risks a lot by supporting you. Mindful of the waves you create."

Carlos nodded, then turned to Ayzili. "Thanks for believing our story." This had been the first time she'd argued in favor of their sanity.

"For now," Ayzili avoided his gaze. She apparently wasn't convinced of her decision. "So where could Zui be hiding?"

"Let's not assume he's hiding," Carlos said. "We just want to talk with him." But deep down, Carlos knew better. Zui was more than just a person of interest; he knew of their trip to the crime scene that night. He must have followed them and overheard their conversation about the garden – a prime suspect for sure.

"Let's see if we can get into the archives," Henry suggested, jogging to catch up with them. Ayzili cast him a look. "What's the problem?" he asked.

"I don't take orders from priests," she said. "Including you."

Hungar smirked. "Still don't trust anyone, Ayzili?"

"Shush," she said, "and stop sulking. These men are here to help you, not replace you, Hungar." She turned back to Carlos. "You think we should start in the gardens?"

"You heard what the lamplighter said before he died."

"That we know of the garden," Ayzili repeated.

"Yeah, although he said it under duress." He gave Ayzili a stern look, but she didn't understand what he meant. Either that, or she didn't care.

Chapter 14

They received a frosty reception at the entrance to the gardens. An elderly priest silently unlocked the doors for them and then sneered over his shoulder as he left. Carlos wasn't surprised. They had accused Zui, a high priest, of complicity in murder. And now they had the gall to search the holy gardens. That made them an enemy of the high priesthood and unwelcome guests here. Well aware of the politics, Hungar had urged them to keep a low profile and only assigned three guards to assist in the search.

"They act like the gardens belong to them," Ayzili said, balling up her fists.

"They don't?" Carlos asked.

Hungar shook his head. "They belong to the city."

"And right now the city belongs to the baka," Ayzili said.

Hungar bristled at her remark. "We're doing all we can."

Sensing the impending argument, Carlos changed the subject. "Let's start at the edges and work our way in. We have a lot of space to cover."

They headed along the outer wall, following it until they arrived at what looked like a Japanese dojo, surrounded by lily-clogged ponds. A tall man emerged from the compound to greet them. Carlos immediately recognized him from the council meeting; it was Sarn, the priest who had argued against them so vehemently. He'd rolled up sleeves, as if he'd been gardening, but there was no sign of a watch on his wrists.

"Ayzili, I see you've brought more of your excellent luck into the city." This time it was Hungar who stepped forward in anger, but Ayzili gently laid a hand on his arm.

"Sarn, don't get in our way," she said.

"You expect I'd stand idle? While non-believers defile the gardens?"

Ayzili kept her voice steady and even. "I don't expect much from you, Sarn. I really don't."

"Yet you wish me dead," Sarn grinned maliciously, "for sending your husband out on expedition."

Ayzili reached for her sword hilt, but Sarn only widened his smile. He seemed to relish the anger he was provoking. However, he still took a step backwards.

"One of our priests had to go - to say the harvest prayer. Believe me, I took no joy in it."

"You took joy," Ayzili whispered under her breath. Carlos could barely hear her finish. "You took all my joy." Her eyes had become wet and fierce. She wiped them on one of her sleeves.

"He supported our cause," Sarn continued, "drafted many new laws, shared our vision of order. By defying me, you dishonor him."

Ayzili walked to within a foot of Sarn and locked eyes with the tall priest. "You may have fooled my husband, but you won't…" She didn't bother to finish her sentence. Instead she turned and addressed the others, "Come on. We've no time for this."

They left the high priest's hermitage and continued along the outer wall. Sarn remained behind and watched them go.

"You owe me a watch," Carlos said, pointing to his wrist.

"Should we start with the garden's torches?" Henry asked. Ayzili glared at him, still smarting from her encounter with Sarn. It made sense that Zui would hide the baka along the torch route; she just wished the suggestion hadn't come from a priest. Carlos could read the hostility on her face.

He scratched his chin, unsure himself of Henry's plan. A half hazard search could miss something. They should do this by the book.

"No," he said, "let's split up into two groups. Work from opposite ends of the gardens." He found a stick and drew a search grid in the dirt. "Zigzag back and forth, hitting each box. We'll rendezvous at the falls."

Hungar nodded and motioned to his guards. "Begin at the herb cottage and work north." Then he turned to the others. "I'm coming with you."

Torch stands dotted the garden's serpentine paths. Eventually they led Hungar, Ayzili, Henry, and Carlos to an old vineyard – rows of latticework interwoven with vines. The noon-day sun shone mercilessly upon the grapes here. Amazingly, the fruit was not dry and shriveled, however, but plump and heavy on the vine. Ayzili plucked one and tossed it into her mouth. The juices ran down her chin as she chewed the seed.

"How's this possible..." Carlos started to ask but stopped when a cool breeze struck him. It whistled through the rows, sending Ayzili's sleeves spinning.

"The library of Ginen," she said, motioning in the direction of the wind.

"That's the archives?" Henry asked. She nodded and led them past the vineyard to the garden wall. Here, an immense gate with wrought iron bars blocked passage down a long, dark corridor. Sunlight didn't penetrate more than a few feet.

"I thought you said there was only one entrance to the Gardens?" Carlos said, resting his hands on the bars. The stream of air made the metal cold to the touch.

"This passageway does not lead out," Ayzili explained. "It leads to the library."

"Are you sure?" Carlos asked. "I'd like to see for myself."

"No," Hungar said, "only ordained members of the priesthood are allowed to enter. We must respect that. After all, the library was built by the lwa."

A convenient excuse, Carlos thought. He wondered if Riyal would grant them an exemption. Better not to play that card yet, he decided. Riyal already risked a lot politically allowing them this search. Carlos stared at a beetle making its way down the corridor. The bug looked like a scarab, but he couldn't be sure.

"Well, I don't know about spirits," he said, "but some folks have been down there recently." Besides the beetle's trail, several shoe prints cut through the dust. One design was quite distinctive, a radiating sun symbol. Carlos made a mental note of its shape and wear pattern.

"How's the library set up?" Henry asked.

Ayzili shrugged. "The Jellyman would love to know. He's been campaigning them for years. But they won't grant him access. Only a few have seen the inside..."

"Those who know, don't tell." Hungar said.

Ayzili laughed. "When we were kids, teachers told us that this is where we'd go when we die. Only dead people down there." She leaned forward and spit her grape seed into the darkness. "There, something for them to eat."

* * *

Henry's feet were killing him, so he took off his sandals.

"Can we stop by that waterfall again? I need to soak these." They'd been searching for several hours now without food, and their stomachs were beginning to rumble.

"Yes, wash those," Ayzili said. "Your feet are ill."

"For my age, they smell pretty good," Henry shot back.

"No, they smell like vomit."

"Easy," Carlos said. "We all stink. Let's take a break."

Being barefoot in the sand was one of Carlos' favorite things, the blisters melting away under shifting grains. Ayzili sat cross-legged beside him, absently drawing designs on the beach. Near the water,

Henry leaned against a rock and flipped through the small book that Jell had lent him. Carlos walked over to his friend and dunked his feet into the water.

"Page turner?"

Henry didn't look up from his book. "Amazing. They matched a saint to each spirit. Look here. Papa Legba, guardian spirit - stands at the crossroads between this world and the next. Recognize the icon?" An image of a Catholic saint clutching a pair of keys filled up most of the page.

"No, I can't say I do."

"Come on. It's St. Peter. The bouncer at the Pearly Gates. Those are the keys to heaven in his hand." He turned the page. "Here's Simbi, the guy this garden's named after. See, I was right about the magi." He tapped on a rendering of three kings, sketched traditionally as if from a nativity scene.

"You'd better watch out," Ayzili said with sarcasm. "Simbi's known to kidnap little kids who play near his springs."

"Is that so?" Henry asked.

Ayzili lowered her voice as if she were telling a ghost story. "He'll keep you prisoner for seven years, but when you're finally released...you'll be given a gift. Like the ability to see the future."

"You believe that?" Carlos asked.

"I believe my parents wanted to keep me from drowning."

Carlos turned thoughtful. "Is that a common story?"

Hungar nodded in agreement. "Yes. They tell it to all the children." He had unpacked a bottle of wine and accompanying shot glasses.

Carlos turned back to look into the cascading sheets of water. In his experience, many rumors on the street had a basis in truth. He'd learned that lesson when he visited his daughter's school in Miami. Several pre-schoolers had told him stories of a monster watching them from the edges of the playground. The monster turned out to be a parole violator with a record of assaulting minors.

There's a lamp-post right here, he realized.

He scanned the beach nearby for markings and found two straight lines dug into the sand...as if a cart had been wheeled right up to the water. Footprints ran parallel to these wheel tracks – the same sunburst pattern he'd seen down the archive corridor. Carlos scratched his chin. He needed to get wet.

"Hungar, can I have two of those glasses?"

"I've brought enough for everyone."

"It's not for drinking." Carlos took the empty glasses and walked to the water's edge. Then he stripped down to his boxers and dove out into the pool. The cold water stung his chest wound, but he ignored the pain.

As he kicked away from the beach, he held the shot glasses to his eyes, forming a makeshift pair of goggles. First thing he noticed was that the pool was much deeper than it appeared. Beneath the bubbling surface, the sand sloped downwards from the beach into a deep basin. Several boulders clustered together in odd formations there, directly beneath the waterfall. They encircled a dark blue opening – the entrance to an underwater cave.

Carlos drifted farther out into the pool to get a better look. One of the boulders beneath him shifted slightly. It was not a boulder. He saw legs, a claw – the baka. It watched him from the cave's entrance, camouflaged against the riverbed like the crawdads he used to hunt in the bayous. But Carlos didn't react; he had to be careful not to betray the fact he'd seen it. The last thing he wanted was scare it off now. To his horror, he realized this was the least of his problems. The baka was rising to meet him. It had pushed off from the bottom and was silently gliding his way, claws open in anticipation.

Oh no, you don't, Carlos thought. He kicked in a causal circle and headed back towards the beach.

Shit. He's coming up fast.

The baka scrambled with all its legs in an effort to reach him. Carlos had no choice but to swim for it. He abandoned subtlety and dropped the shot glasses. His legs pumped violently, but to no avail. A current generated by the falls slowed his speed significantly. The baka would be on him in seconds. Cresting the surface he cried out one word, "Baka." Then he felt an intense jolt of pain as a claw yanked him below the waterline.

Carlos felt his ears pop as the baka dragged him deeper. He heard a splash, saw an explosion of bubbles, and realized the others had dove in after him. He glanced down at the baka, its eyes grossly magnified by the water. One claw had clamped around his sandal. The other tried to snag his free leg. Carlos kicked wildly and connected with the shell. The baka must have realized it had bit off more than it could chew, for it let go and fled back into the depths.

Ayzili pressed after it, but she couldn't keep up. Underwater, she was no match for the crab, its physique better suited for the depths. Already the baka was disappearing into the blurry darkness. Soon, it would be gone forever. Ayzili pinched her nose and puffed out her cheeks, but it was clear she couldn't equalize. Hungar, on the other hand, didn't seem affected by the pressure.

Weighted down by his armor, he kicked past her with a few powerful strokes and landed between the crab and cave. The baka reeled back in shock, its escape now blocked. Then it straightened, no longer afraid. Hungar sensed movement behind him and spun around.

The darkness of the cave shifted. Something moved just beyond its rim, something large. A monstrous creature unfolded its legs, brandished its pincers, and stepped out from the shadows. Hungar slowly looked up and into the eyes of a towering grey baka.

The creature's shell was encrusted with thousands of white diamonds, all interconnected by a spider web of veves that gave testament to the dozens of men it had killed.

Ayzili frantically waved at Hungar, gesturing for him to swim away. But Hungar stood his ground. Slowly, he reached for his sword and gripped the hilt. The Quartermaster stepped forward. The diamonds sparkled as sunlight struck them.

It's beautiful, Carlos thought.

The silt coating the riverbed erupted as the baka surged forward. Its claws thrashed up a sandstorm, instantly enveloping Hungar. And just like that, he was gone.

* * *

Ayzili and Henry helped Carlos to the shore. Although his foot was sore, the sandal had thankfully taken the brunt of the pinch.

"Hurry, it'll follow us," Ayzili gasped.

Carlos stumbled upon the beach. "What was that?"

"A Quartermaster. Here he comes."

Everyone turned back to the falls. The pool below was no longer a deep, cerulean blue but an inky black. A shadow rose from the deep. It crested the surface, sending rivulets of water running in every direction. Two red eyes stared back at them.

"No." Ayzili whispered, once she realized the creature was chewing on something. "Oh no. Please no."

The baka crawled halfway out of the water, a human leg dangling from its jaws. Henry gagged.

"You bastard." Ayzili could barely hold back the tears. Her last words to Hungar had been said in anger. And now it was too late to make amends. He was dead.

"Go." Ayzili dove onto the sand, somersaulting away with exaggerated movements. She was obviously trying to draw the baka's attention, and it worked. The crab shifted towards her and swung out with its claws. They sliced into the sand, narrowly missing her legs. She reached into the roots of an Elm, where she'd hidden her poison dagger. The blade whizzed through the air and ricocheted harmlessly off the baka's shell, inches from one of its eyes.

“Run, she yelled. The baka’s next blow sideswiped Ayzili, sending her tumbling backwards into the hibiscus. The creature then shifted back to Carlos and Henry.

It hauled itself onto the beach and towered above them, water dripping off its legs, feelers in its mouth twitching madly. With speed Carlos did not think possible, the baka shot out one of its claws. The serrated pincers closed around Henry’s leg and hoisted him high into the air.

Carlos screamed in anger. But all he could do was watch helplessly as his friend neared the baka’s mouth, a grinding hell of salivating mandibles. A whooshing sound breezed past his ear. Something connected with the creature’s shell and fell to the sand below: an arrow.

Carlos glanced up to see the sky filled with hundreds of narrow shafts. They whizzed through the air and bounced harmlessly off the creature’s thick hide. Still more sliced through the leaves overhead. The baka let out a great cry. Several of the arrows had struck the tender area around its mouth. The creature dropped Henry to the pool below, snapped wildly at air, and then toppled backwards into the shallows. It spun around in the pool, dove beneath the surface, and disappeared under the falls. Sarn emerged from behind a palmetto with quiver in hand. A dozen archers in priestly robes followed behind him.

“You’re lucky to be alive,” he told them matter-of-factly. One of the priests helped Ayzili back onto the beach. Blood matted up her hair and ran down her face. Several others tended to Henry’s leg.

“Did you know about this baka?” Carlos asked angrily.

"No. We most certainly did not."

Ayzili pushed the priests off her. "No others killed?" she asked.

"Killed?" Sarn spotted a sandal on the beach. His face flashed the hint of a smile. But it instantly vanished as he turned back to them. "Hungar was a great warrior," he said at last.

"There's a tunnel down there," Carlos said. "That's how the baka have been entering the city."

"If that's true, then we will seal it," Sarn said too quickly. "Come. You can recover from your wounds at the hermitage."

"I'd rather bleed to death." Ayzili pulled free of their grasps and yanked Carlos to his feet. "We're leaving. These gardens are home to demons."

Chapter 15

Back in the city, the Jellyman quickly ushered them off the street and into his study. Carlos could tell by the look on his face that he already knew what had happened. Word traveled fast in this city.

"I'm sorry to hear about Hungar," he said to Ayzili. She nodded wearily and collapsed into a wicker chair.

"The priesthood knew about the tunnel," she said through clenched teeth. "I know they did. They let the baka in."

"Maybe," Carlos said, "but then why did they save us? Conspiracy's tough to prove. Here's what we do know; whoever picked up the baka at the waterfall also visited the archive. I matched a shoe print at both places. We should ask who visited the archive recently. It could've been Zui acting alone...but I doubt it."

He knew it went well beyond Zui and the lamplighter. These were foot soldiers, not masterminds. They had just scratched the surface of something deeper. And now came the hard part - finding the leaders. Carlos had once testified at a corruption case internal affairs had dug up in Miami. Drugs went missing from the evidence locker.

A few officers ended up taking the fall for those running the show. The masterminds were never disciplined. Unraveling this conspiracy could prove equally difficult.

"Let's see where the evidence leads us," he said. "I'd like to speak with Sasha's father. Find out who knew she was alone." He sighed and examined the bruise on his foot. It felt better after he'd loosened the sandal. Henry, however, was in much worse shape. Blood stained the bandages the priests had applied to his leg, but at least the bleeding had stopped. He hobbled about on a staff that Jell had given him.

"Her father's here tonight," Jell said. "Come, they're waiting for us in the peristyle. We've much to discuss." Henry groaned. Right now all he wanted to do was sleep.

The group crossed the courtyard into the pavilion where they had confronted the assassin the previous night. Candles illuminated the space and cast flickering shadows on those gathered there. It was a large crowd, every bench filled, but the chatter silenced immediately once they'd entered.

Jell addressed the crowd, quickly bringing everyone up to date on the discovery in the gardens and its implications. "The balance of power is shifting. In light of these baka attacks, Sarn has moved quickly to abolish the council and remove Riyal from power. He wants the high priesthood to take full authority." Murmurs of disapproval rumbled through those gathered.

"And the city guard?" asked Carlos. "Will they allow this?"

"Most of them support the high priesthood. They share a strict view of the law. Only Hungar's leadership distanced them and now that he's gone, they're sure to form an alliance. Together they're a formidable power."

Carlos thought of his wristwatch. The ties between the high priesthood and city guards went deeper than he'd suspected. Much was happening behind the scenes. And these attacks were the perfect excuse for Sarn's cabal to take power. That alone was motive enough for him to side with the baka, orchestrate the killings, and bribe the city guard to look the other way.

But has Sarn really crossed that line? Or is he just a political opportunist? Carlos knew only factions of these groups might be responsible. He shouldn't jump to conclusions, accusing everyone in fit of McCarthyism.

Maybe Sarn was simply acting out of desperation, like an animal backed into a corner. After the discovery of the baka tunnel in the gardens, Sarn knew the high priesthood might loose popular support. So he'd made a desperate grab for power before he lost it all. Carlos shook his head. He needed solid proof before he could clear or convict anyone.

Ayzili cursed behind him.

"Their laws won't protect us. They'll tie our hands while the baka feast."

"That's why we stand against them." Jell motioned to the figures gathered in the room. A few were dressed in the tan robes of the local priests like Jell. Others wore simple vests and tunics.

"Let me introduce our new friends." Jell's voice echoed off the high ceiling. "This is Father Henry McKraggen and Carlos Consuelo...the ones who cracked the baka's secret."

A man in a thick jacket with a thicker mustache emerged from the crowd and embraced Carlos. He was short but quite muscular and blazed with intensity.

"I'm Moro, Sasha's father." The man looked directly into Carlos' eyes with an unwavering stare. "Thank you for finding the baka that murdered my daughter."

"I'm sorry we weren't able to kill it."

"So am I. But you saved others from enduring her fate."

Carlos tried to get a read on the man, but his face was stone, no hint of emotion. Moro either excelled at repressing his grief or had none to show. To find out which, Carlos needed to speak with him further, but not here. They had to be alone. This was an important interview; Moro had a key to his house and would likely know who else had access.

"We must take the next move," Jell said, addressing the crowd. "It's obvious factions of this city conspired to let the baka in. The high priesthood will ignore this to save face. But we can't afford to do that."

"It'll be hard to tell who's involved," Carlos said. "No one's going to admit their guilt freely. We'll need proof."

"And you shall find it." A man in faded robes stepped from the shadows and lowered his hood. It was Riyal, the council elder who'd granted them access to the gardens. "You will find those responsible," he said evenly.

Riyal could have whispered if he'd wanted to, for the room had instantly silenced. Few apparently realized he was here among them, and a reverent hush filled the chamber. Jell stood dumbfounded.

"For years I wondered why the baka allowed our city to remain, when all others had fallen," Riyal said. "Only now do I understand the ancient text." He paused to visualize the passage, before continuing. "Evil men shall hide in shadow, giving the baka strength. But they cannot hide forever. Strangers from the west will reveal the city's cancer. This has come to pass."

He glanced at Carlos and then began to pace. "Those who let the baka in, did so out of fear and greed; fear for their own skins and greed for the wealth the baka could provide. They thought not of the victims."

Jell finally found his voice, "They think they can save themselves by sacrificing a few of us."

"My daughter has died," Moro said coldly. "She made no sacrifice. It was murder."

One of the other priests spoke up, "If this betrayal is true, then the baka have gained strength. Our city will fall."

"Our city's already fallen," Ayzili spoke from the corner. "We're nothing but food to them. And I, for one, would rather die from a swift blow than bleed to death from within."

Carlos shook his head, the image of a lobster tank coming to mind. Ayzili was right. Ginen served as food storage for these creatures – the mere illusion of safety. A dawning comprehension hit him. "Now that we've prevented the baka from sneaking into the city, they'll attack from outside, won't they? How many?"

"Many thousands," Riyal said. "A dozen for every each man, woman, and child in all of Ginen. I imagine they're already amassing their forces."

"Then we've got to get ready for them," Carlos said. Henry twisted around to look at his friend. He'd not heard such conviction in Carlos's voice since his daughter's passing.

A slight smile returned to Riyal's lips. His eyes crinkled as if he'd been waiting many years to hear those words. "We'll need poison," he said at last. "Moro, how much was gathered on your last expedition?"

Moro was lost in his thought and had to be nudged. Maybe the loss of his daughter has affected him after all, Carlos thought.

"Yamala? Oh, a miserable crop. We barely filled a single bladder," Moro said distractedly. "The baka sentries destroyed the fish before we could get to them. They knew we were coming, knew our every move."

Riyal frowned. "Then you must launch another, longer-range expedition at once. Take as many hands as can be spared." Intentional or not, his eyes bore right into Carlos as he spoke these last few words. "We have but a few short days before the onslaught."

"We'll leave before sunrise," said Jell.

Riyal put a hand on his shoulder. "Jell, you should stay to spread the word. We must prepare for war against the baka. I'll help as well, but the high priests are making my life difficult. They'll think I'm building an army to overthrow them. So, they may imprison me."

The room instantly exploded into conversation, with most people in support of Riyal's plan. Henry put his fingers together and gave a sharp whistle. The sound immediately silenced the boisterous crowd.

"Listen, this doesn't have to be a last stand." He gestured to Carlos. "We can lead you back to our home...a place much safer than this. We marked the walls on our way out."

Only silence greeted his words. Abandoning Ginen wasn't an idea anyone had considered. Riyal stepped forward to explain why.

"I'm afraid," the old man said, "that's not so easy. The baka guard their nest jealously. We could never get a large group through."

Henry crossed his arms, clearly unconvinced. Carlos knew his friend would never abandon those in need. It went against everything for which he stood. Either they all escaped or none of them did. Reluctantly, Henry nodded in agreement; he'd stay.

"Yes, we should consider alternatives," Riyal continued, "but meanwhile, prepare for the coming siege. Moro, you and the others must ready another expedition and depart as soon as you're able."

Once the group had dissolved into separate conversation, Riyal grabbed Carlos by the elbow. "Can we talk alone for a moment?" He led Carlos outside to one of the concrete skirts that collared the lemon trees.

"Thank you for discovering the truth about the gardens."

Carlos shook his head. "I think I've barely scratched the surface."

Riyal nodded, then lowered his voice. "The evil runs deeper than any of us imagine. They've planted spies everywhere, saboteurs at the highest levels." He glanced over his shoulder to make sure they weren't overheard. "Five of the last expeditions have met with failure. We've taken measures, but the baka are always a step ahead."

"How so?"

"An expedition member must be leaking information, alerting the baka of our position and movements. Once they hear we're on the march, the creatures hurry ahead and destroy the yamala before we can harvest it. That's the only explanation."

"So you want me to tag along and find the traitor?"

Riyal smiled, the wrinkles in his face accentuated by the torchlight. "This expedition must succeed. If we don't replenish our poison stock, we'll never outlast a siege."

Carlos nodded. "I'll do the best I can."

"This task is a dangerous one, you realize."

"I understand that," Carlos said. "I've been through tough scrapes before."

"Good." Riyal patted his shoulder and stood up. "I should get back inside. Jell will think I've picked a new favorite." He smiled and shuffled back into the crowd. As Carlos watched him go, he noticed that Henry had been waiting in the wings for them to finish.

"This is getting out of hand," Henry said, walking up to him. "We're in the middle of a civil war."

"No, Riyal's more concerned with saving the city, than returning to power."

"Saving the city?" Henry ran both hands through his hair. "The city's lost, Carlos. If there's really that many creatures out there, this place isn't safe. We've got to convince everyone to flee to the Brac."

"The whole city?" Carlos sighed. "Including the children and elderly? You know they'd never make it. No, the best thing we can do for these folks is help them uncover the traitors."

"Is that the best thing for them or for you?"

"What are you talking about?"

"We're not Woodward & Bernstein." Henry said, his face starting to fluster. "It could take years to unravel this conspiracy. And even then, you may not get everyone. You've got to let this go."

Carlos ignored his pessimism. "This isn't about me."

Henry brought his voice under control. "I'm your friend, Carlos. And I know how you get. Last time you lost your job, your wife...briefly your sanity - all in pursuit of these ghosts that could never be caught. I'm not letting you do that again."

Carlos shrugged. "Well, it's not up to you. An expedition's leaving tomorrow, and I'm tagging along. Riyal thinks there's a traitor amongst them."

"Are you serious?" He waited for Carlos to crack a smile. When he didn't, Henry threw his hands in the air. "You've got no experience fighting crabs. This is going to get you killed."

Privately, Carlos did wonder if he'd become blind to the risks, consumed with the girl's murder and catching those responsible. But nothing Henry could say now would change his mind; nothing could make him abandon this investigation. He knew very well the dark places this might lead. The memories of Miami were painfully fresh. But he was set on a path and determined to see it through to the end. It was the way he'd always operated, and he wasn't about to change now.

"We've got a chance to root them out. This narrows our pool of suspects. If we can catch one of the traitor's alive and turn him...."

Henry's face showed he wasn't convinced. "Well, I'm in no condition to go on any expedition."

"But you can dig around here."

Henry rolled his eyes and said nothing. Carlos knew this was a lot to ask of his friend. But as he'd said, they were here for a reason. He wasn't going to run and hide from death. Not this time. Out of the corner of his eye, he saw Ayzili leave the peristyle and slip past them. "Excuse me," he said. "I'll be right back."

Henry shook his finger. "We're not done here."

"Exactly," Carlos said as he walked farther into the schoolyard.

"No, I mean this conversation —"

He caught up with Ayzili near a mapou tree, her silhouette striking in the moonlight. When Carlos saw her face, however, the image of confidence shattered. Her lips were drawn, eyes glazed, and forehead strained as if a terrible weight pressed upon her. It took all his strength to break the silence.

"Sides have been drawn, eh? I'll go with the expedition. But Henry should stay to heal. He can help Jell."

She turned and looked at him with moist eyes. "It's the final days of Ginen. You shouldn't die with us."

"You don't think we can fight them?"

"Oh, we can fight them. As long as there's breath in my lungs I'll fight. But we can't kill them, not all of them." She plucked a lemon and began picking at its skin.

"If we arm everyone —" Carlos began but she silenced him with a look.

"You've seen an infant, a sentry, and a quartermaster. There are things beneath the sand much worse than these, worse than you could ever imagine." Ayzili tossed the lemon into the darkness.

Carlos locked eye with her. "Tell me."

"There's much we don't know." She tucked a few strands of hair behind her ear. "But I've seen plenty."

She explained how baka traveled in regiments, each headed by a quartermaster, who supplied the rest with food. Other baka served different roles: foot soldiers did the heavy lifting, sentries guarded the caves, skimmers were the messengers. Then there were the climbers, water bearers, and even tunnelers. Ayzili had obviously devoted the last few years to studying these creatures. They were numerous, and they were intelligent.

She counted off the different baka on her fingers. Then balled them into fists. "There are countless others I haven't placed yet. I've seen baka that would make your skin crawl."

"I saw diamonds on that last one."

Ayzili nodded. "Baka are vain. They decorate their shells with gems. Quartermasters prefer diamonds. The terrible ones choose rubies."

It was a lot to take in. Carlos gazed up at the moon; he didn't recognize the craters anymore.

"You'll see soon enough," she half whispered. He looked back at her face. Genuine fear shown in her eyes – the first time she'd revealed it. If she were afraid, he knew it was for a good reason. At that moment, he felt a great need to tell her about his daughter. He couldn't explain it, but the words pulled at his tongue, begging to be spoken. Right then, he wanted to tell her everything.

Instead he whispered, "You think we'll die in the fight?"

She frowned, and her grave expression deepened. "That's the least of my worries."

Chapter 16

Henry and Carlos went to bed early, leaving their conversation unresolved. They'd been friends so long, each knew what the other would say. But this is different from Miami, Carlos thought. Back then he let emotion cloud his mind. He wouldn't become obsessed this time. He'd use solid police work to get justice for this little girl. And going on this expedition was simply the next logical step. He needed to find the mole and turn him, get him to talk. Deep down, Carlos suspected something else was driving him, but he didn't want to go there. He'd fled to the Brac just to escape those dark thoughts.

The expedition party gathered in the early light. They numbered well over fifty men, armed aggressively with all manners of swords, arrows, and spears. Ayzili surveyed the group.

"No priests, eh? Who's going to say the prayers?"

"You'll have to skip those," Jell said, ignoring her sarcasm. "The local priests need to stay here and spread the word to the city. We can't fight the baka alone."

"Then I guess the high priests haven't sanctioned us," Ayzili said, laughing. She stretched out her calves as if eager to begin the trek.

"How far are you traveling?" Henry asked the group. This was the first time he'd spoken all morning, still smarting from their argument the previous night.

Sasha's father, Moro, approached them. "Several days at least, to find a fresh supply. We'll hug the coast so the tide can clean our tracks."

"Are you sure the baka won't attack before we return?" Carlos asked him.

"That's a chance we have to take."

Ayzili smiled. "Don't worry....we'll meet our share in the wild."

Carlos nodded grimly and then turned to Henry. "I'm sorry. This is just something I have to do."

Henry managed a weak smile. "Ok, but how will you know when you've done it?"

"When I've caught everyone who had a hand in that girl's death."

Henry sighed. "That might never happen, Carlo."

"Then I'll give it a damn good try."

"Just don't get yourself killed in the process." Henry reached out and embraced him. "Godspeed," he said. "I'll keep my eyes open around here." Carlos was glad his friend didn't hold a grudge. He wanted to part on good terms.

"I told you not to go surfing."

"Haha...you bastard." Henry waved goodbye as the party marched through the gates.

Outside Ginen, the wind blew fiercely. Carlos grimaced. Sand grains stung his eyes for a good half mile, until he followed the other men's example and wrapped his face in cloth. The expedition party quickly made their way towards the water, where the sand was wetter and did not fly about as much. Monstrous waves crashed in the distance, which made Carlos glad that Henry hadn't joined them. He'd find some way to go surfing.

The group trudged along single file at a fast clip. Walking on the hard sand was going to give him blisters, Carlos knew. To ignore the pain, his mind started to wander. It went back to the place it always went, the shores of Miami.

His daughter's sandcastle was almost finished, and he sat back to admire it.

"Nice work, Violet" he said, snapping a shot with his camera. She wasn't pleased. Even though she'd laid driftwood support rods, the towers still weren't high enough, and they lacked decoration. "The tide's coming in, sweetie. We should work on the wall."

She ignored him, however, and continued layering seaweed onto the towers. Then, using a seashell, she carved a balcony into its side.

Carlos set down his shovel. "Those decorations aren't going to last if the wall fails."

Violet cast him a sour look, one that always packed on the guilt. She must've learned it from her mother.

"The castle's going to drown?" she asked with hurt in her voice.

Carlos shaded his vision and took note of the high water mark left by driftwood. It was well beyond the sandcastle, far up the beach.

"No, sweetie...your castle's going to survive." He dug in deep and packed more wet sand against the wall. The waves crashed louder behind them now. Carlos smiled and straightened his daughter's hair. Her wig had gone askew.

Something crunched beneath his feet.

Carlos lifted a sandal. The pale circle of a sand dollar lay pressed inside his footprint. He reached down and picked it up.

"That's a good omen," Moro said, taking it from him. "They call this the ghost shell." He pointed to its design. "See the flower? That's the lily that grows in the gardens." He ran his finger across the shape. "This hole near the center is our city, Ginen."

"What are these other holes?" Carlos asked, pointing to four others that were spaced outside the flower design.

"Those were the other cities," Moro said. A wistfulness in his voice told Carlos not to enquire further. "Before the sands shifted, before the baka." Pressing into the sand dollar with his thumbs, he broke it in half. Then he gently shook the pieces over his outstretched palm. Five broken fragments fell into his hand. They looked like birds. "These are five lwa who will save us, when our world splits apart." Moro smiled for the first time and let the birds slip thru his fingers into the sand. A rush of water swept in and consumed them. "The tide is rising," he said. "We should angle towards the dunes." But Carlos grabbed his shoulder.

"Can I ask you something?"

Moro turned back around. "You want to know what kind of a father would leave his daughter alone?"

Carlos swallowed hard, caught off guard by the comment. For a moment, he thought Moro's question was directed at him. But the guilty expression on the man's face told him otherwise. "No, I'm not here to judge you. I want to know about the key."

"To my house?"

"Yes, they found one on your daughter. Was that the only one?"

"No, I've got one as well." He removed it from his pocket. "But I had it with me the whole time I was away." He gave it to Carlos, who inspected it closely for signs of wax. The handle was clean, however, ending in a beautiful flowering design.

"Was it ever out of your possession, even for a little while?"

Moro's eyes narrowed. He saw where Carlos was going with this. "Yes, a week ago. When I had it copied for Sasha."

"You had it copied?" Carlos scratched his chin. "Who did that for you?"

Moro grit his teeth. "The city guard." His hand curled around the hilt of his sword, but he did not withdraw it.

"Why them?" Carlos asked.

"They handle all the lock work in the city."

Someone could have easily made a third key and used it to enter the house that night. Carlos had a feeling this was a dead end, literally. With Hungar's death, he had no access to the city guard. And they weren't likely to implicate one of their own.

"You think there were others besides the lamplighter?" Moro asked, "...responsible?"

"Yes, I do. And I think one of them might be traveling with us."

Moro nodded as if he'd suspected this as well. "Many think the baka can read the future...can predict our actions. But that's a lie. They're being fed information." He lowered his voice. "On our last expedition, we changed direction mid-route, but still they beat us to the harvest."

"The fact they didn't attack you is also suspicious," Carlos said. "It points to a spy in your midst, someone they didn't want to kill."

"Anyway I can help, you let me know." Moro's eyes welled with tears.

"I will." Carlos asked a few more questions, but they didn't provide anything of use. By the rise in Moro's voice, he could tell the man was becoming upset, so he decided to end the interview. Moro was clearly wrestling with his emotions: a dangerous cocktail of guilt, anger, and sadness. The stone face he'd exhibited the other night was not apathy, but merely his public mask. Behind this was devastation, utter despair. Carlos understood only too well.

As the group marched into softer sand, he drifted towards the back of the line, lost again in his thoughts. Soon he'd fallen away from the others with nothing behind him but a long trail of footprints. Carlos stared down at these tracks as he walked. Then he stopped.

I've seen that before.

He was looking at a familiar print in the sand, a radiating sun pattern. Instantly, he knew where he recognized it from - the gardens. This was the same print he'd observed down the locked archive corridor. More disturbingly, he'd also seen it near the cart tracks by the waterfall, which meant it likely belonged to the traitor.

Or maybe it's just the same pattern on a different sandal, Carlos told himself. That was certainly possible. But he wasn't buying it. One of the rings had a chip missing. He'd seen that wear pattern before; it was too much of a coincidence. This was the exact same sandal.

Riyal's fears had proven correct. Someone inside the expedition party was conspiring with the baka and leaking information on their whereabouts.

Should I stop the march and ask to see everyone's sandals? No, he needed to be more discreet. He'd wait until they made camp. Playing his cards close to his chest seemed like the best strategy for now - at least until he'd gathered more evidence. He still had to figure out how the spy was leaking information, and if there were more than one traitor in their midst.

Chapter 17

After the expedition departed, Henry and Jell walked back through the streets alone. Without Carlos to intervene, Henry felt he could finally ask some theological questions. He'd do it diplomatically of course, with his usual charm.

"Beside these spirits..." he began, "do you serve a higher power?"

Jell smiled. "You don't trust those who serve the lwa?"

Henry knew he was treading on dangerous ground. Carlos had been right to keep him from starting this conversation. "No," he put his hands up in a gesture of apology, "I'm just trying to understand the differences."

"There are thousands of ways to serve the lwa." Jell slowed his pace so that Henry could catch up. His leg injury forced him to limp, and he leaned heavily on the staff.

"Our ways are quite different," Henry said.

Jell smiled. "They're paths to the same place."

Be that as it may, Henry thought, some paths are more direct than others. "So you believe in God?" he asked.

"Yes, Bondeye."

"Is that another spirit?" They approached the entrance to the orphanage. Jell took his keys out and began to unlock the door.

"Bondeye is God. He's not a lwa."

Before Henry could follow up, the door swung open. A tall, balding man greeted them with a spoon in one hand. Jell introduced him as one of the teachers.

"Breakfast is ready," the bald man said, stepping aside, "and you have a guest." Looking past him, Henry was surprised to see Riyal, the ex-leader of the council, sitting at the table. Jell looked equally dumbstruck.

"Welcome, sir. Had I know you were coming I..." He smoothed the tangles in his beard.

"I can't stay long." Riyal's eyes were bloodshot and weighed down with fatigue. It was clear he hadn't been sleeping well. "Has the expedition left safely?"

"Yes, half an hour ago."

"No trouble from anyone?"

"Were you expecting any?"

Riyal frowned and motioned to the chairs. "Be careful whom you trust out there. Allies of the baka are numerous."

"Would you like some milk?" the bald teacher asked and offered him a mug. Riyal accepted it gratefully and downed the contents in one swig. Then he took a deep breath.

"The council's been disbanded." He pinched his nose and closed his eyes as if suffering from a migraine. "The high priesthood took control this morning."

"With the blessing of the city guard?" Jell asked.

Riyal nodded. "They think locking down the city will solve everything. But it won't stop the invasion. At this point, nothing will." He sighed deeply. "Now their eyes are on me, awaiting my next move. They mean to arrest me." He rested a hand on Jell's arm. "So it's up to you to spread the warning. Don't go to council members, too many rest in Sarn's pocket."

"We'll visit the Baron and the twins today," Jell said, then caught the look of confusion on Henry's face. "They're strong voices in the other quarters," he explained. "We'll need their support to defend Ginen. - to build an army."

"They should arm themselves and gather supplies. We must band together as one city, for we cannot do this alone. Let's hope they'll listen." Riyal eyes darted back and forth. "Lines have been drawn in the sand. If Sarn wins, if we do nothing, then we will certainly die."

"Why does Sarn ignore the threat?" Henry asked.

"Either he's a fool, or worse…" Riyal bowed his head, darkly. The implication was clear; Sarn likely conspired with the baka. But without proof, Riyal wouldn't make the accusation. He spotted Henry's book on the lwa and his wrinkles softened. "You're reading about the mysteries?"

It took Henry a moment to realize he was being addressed. "Me? Oh yes, just doing some research."

The old man arched an eyebrow. "You've befriended a fellow scholar, eh Jell? Well, you'll find answers in those pages, Father, believe me. I've been searching myself." He cracked a knowing smile.

"You know what book I rely on the most?" Henry asked. He decided a soft sell would be the most effective. "The Bible."

Riyal nodded, apparently familiar with scripture. Then he locked a stare on Henry. "In the archive, one phrase keeps popping up." He turned thoughtful for a moment. "Five lwa will lead you...what does that mean?" His voice trailed off, as if reading from some forgotten manuscript in his mind. "Maybe you'll discover what I've been searching for all these many years."

"What's that?"

"The way to save Ginen," Riyal whispered and then produced, from the folds of his robes, a small, tightly wrapped present. An intricate web of green and purple cloth had been woven around the gift with feathers sprouting from its top, making it resemble a cross between an onion and a peacock. "Here, take this paquet. May it bring you luck." He placed the charm firmly on the table. Then he winked and pulled the hood over his head.

Why does everyone give me these things? Henry wondered, inspecting the charm. The craftsmanship was exquisite, far more elaborate than Mambo's gift. Henry considered Riyal's words. What did he mean by saving Ginen? Henry had a feeling he wasn't talking about eternal salvation, but something more literal.

"Will you stay for breakfast?" Jell asked but Riyal had already left. The bald teacher who had served them also moved to the door.

"I've some errands to do," he said brusquely and turned to leave.

Jell gave him a disapproving look. "No one eats a full breakfast anymore."

After downing a few biscuits and redressing the bandages around Henry's foot, the two set off into the city. With a shrill whistle, Jell halted an elderly man drawing a carriage and talked him into a ride. Soon, they were rumbling along the streets and alleyways at a decent clip.

Henry clung tightly to his seat. "Explain the different quarters to me again?" he asked.

"Ginen is divided into four sections. The council and high priests lie in the north, high in the tower and gardens. That's just beyond here." Jell pointed up and behind them. "We'll visit the other quarters today, where most of the people live."

"And who are we speaking with?"

"People of influence. Those with connections."

The Jellyman turned his attention to the driver and began to speak in a language Henry didn't recognize. Rather than watch the streets roll by, Henry decided to study his lwa book more carefully.

It wasn't much more than a list of spirits, a simple schoolbook. He wondered if Riyal was joking when he said the key to saving Ginen lay within its pages. And what did he mean when he said that five lwa would lead them? Maybe this was a parable, some allegorical story that revealed the baka's weakness.

Try to look at it like a sermon, he thought. The puzzle pieces were spread out; he just had to put them together and create a picture that makes sense.

Henry thumbed through the pages. Each one was dedicated to a single spirit or lwa. This was announced in a bold typeface that ran across the top. Flipping through, Henry didn't recognize any of the names - Agwe, Ogoun, Ghede - but he did recognize the portraits. An image of Catholic saint lay beneath each name. Their corresponding symbol, what Jell called veves, was also listed. The current page revealed the Virgin Mary's symbol to be a checked cross with a dagger in it.

This spirit was called Ayzili, same as their fierce warrior friend. Her parents must've had a sense of humor; she certainly was a heartbreaker. Henry skimmed the background information: patron saint of mothers, likes salted pork, the color red, and is obsessed with knives. The human Ayzili seemed to share these tastes, especially the affinity for blades.

Strange to name your daughter after a spirit. He wondered if any other citizens of Ginen had such personal connections with their patron saints? His gut told him this was important, he just didn't know why. So he asked Jell about it.

"The lwa who guides you - they are known as your met tet," Jell answered. "You see the character of a person, is the character of his lwa."

Henry vaguely remembered Carlos saying something about this. “So people choose the…” he searched for the right word, “guardian angel that best matches them?

“No, the spirit chooses us…even you have one.”

It dawned on Henry the extent of this spiritual connection. They thought everyone had a patron saint, one deeply linked to their personality and profession. He wondered which one Jell claimed.

Before he could ask, Jell motioned ahead. “We’re almost there.”

“Where’s there?” Henry asked.

“The graveyard.”

Chapter 18

"Over there's where they buried Sasha last night," the Jellyman pointed sadly. He gestured across a vast expanse of whitewashed mausoleums that stretched to the outer wall of Ginen.

"Is everyone buried above ground?" Henry asked.

"Oh no. Those are for the living."

Henry scratched his beard. "I thought you said this was the graveyard?"

"It is."

"You mean people live on top of the graveyard?"

Jell nodded. "Refugees from the fallen cities. This is the only place for them." He smiled at Henry's reaction and then led the way up a street paved with flat panels, the names of the deceased freshly carved upon them.

The cemetery soon gave rise to small hill. At its peak, Henry saw a modest house with a cross rising from its roof. Arriving at the door, Jell knocked twice and then waited.

"Up here," came a horse cry from above. "Come in."

Jell swung open the door to reveal a barren room void of comfortable furniture. All it contained was a single table, scattering of chairs, and a shelf stocked with black candles and purple lilies. An intricate mural caught Henry's eye on the far wall: a morose assemblage of coffins and tombstones.

"The baron lives like a monk," Jell said, "but he sure doesn't act like one." A ray of light fell from an opening in the ceiling, apparently the entrance to the roof. Jell started climbing the ladder that was propped up against it.

They crested the ceiling and stepped out onto the roof deck. Henry shielded his eyes against the glare. In one corner, he saw a thin, elderly man sitting crossed legged on a canvas deck chair, aligned to the sun. He wore a navy jacket and Lincoln-esque top hat, one size too small. Dark sunglasses covered his lean, sunken face – and for a moment Henry wondered if he might be dead.

"Baron Crux, we need to talk."

"Is that you, Jellyman?" the sleeping man asked. His voice sounded pinched and nasal, as if he spoke through the nose.

"Yes. Riyal bade me speak with you."

"Can't the old fool do it himself? Or are his bones too weak to climb up here? Hah." The Baron leaned forward to get a better look at his new guests. "Who's that with you?"

"This is Father Henry McKraggen, one of the strangers you've likely heard about."

At this introduction, Crux rose to his feet, a smile crossing his thin lips.

"Aha. So you're the one who tried to save that little girl's soul? Please have a drink with me. And welcome to my Southern Cemetery." He gestured to the neighborhood below.

The ladder rattled behind them and soon a woman climbed into view. Her face gave Henry a shock, for she was strikingly beautiful but in a creepy way: middle-aged with strong cheekbones and raven black hair that contrasted strongly with her pale complexion. The skin was so drained of color, it looked as if she'd recently drowned. This couple definitely fits their cemetery surroundings, he thought.

"Geesh, woman," said Crux. "You look like you crawled from the crypt."

"I did," she snapped, "and it was your turn to clean it." Her head ducked back into the house.

"Please pardon my wife's temper. She's always bitter due to her sagging breasts."

"I heard that," came a voice from below, "and they're not the only things sagging around here."

As they descended the creaking ladder, the woman stared at them with arms crossed.

"This is Bridgette, my wife," Crux said affectionately.

"Who's the stranger?" she asked, and again Jell made introductions. Hearing them, Bridgette simply snorted and then retreated into the kitchen to make drinks. Crux motioned for them to take a seat. Even though they were out of bright sun, he kept on his hat and glasses, which reminded Henry of Mrs. Sutherland back on the Brac...if Mrs. Sutherland were a dirty old man.

"So, what does the old fool want this time?" Crux asked.

"I wish you wouldn't call him that," Jell started but was cut off.

"I'll call him whatever I please. I'm not going to kiss the sandals of a council member."

"Well, Riyal's no longer on the council. The high priesthood and city guards have taken power."

This bit of news didn't seem to surprise Crux. "I heard as much," he said simply.

"You know as well as I that they'll ignore the gathering threat. They might use it as an excuse to control the city, but in the end, they won't protect us."

"What gathering threat is that?" Crux asked, baiting him.

Jell's face flushed red. "The baka's tunnel has been discovered. With no easy way to feed upon our young, they'll want to finish us off. A major attack is imminent." He looked imploringly at his reflection in their host's dark glasses. "Your society must draw up arms and help us defend the city."

At that moment, Bridgette arrived bearing a pitcher of some drink Henry didn't recognize: tiny red peppers floating about a clear liquid. She set it down along with a basket of grilled peanuts and then pulled up a chair for herself. Crux poured himself a glass and took a deep slug.

"Who's to say the baka will attack?" he said at last.

"Of course they will. We've cut off their access. We have to prepare for war."

"Maybe this preparation will be what provokes them." Crux poured a glass for Henry and slid it over to him.

"I don't follow," said Henry.

"Ginen is the only city the baka haven't destroyed, the only one. Don't hear me wrong, I'm glad that tunnel was discovered. The killings had to stop. But if the baka see us stocking weapons, if they see us fortifying our defenses – we'll only be encouraging them. We'll be the ones starting the war."

Henry shook his head. He couldn't see the logic in this. "So, you'll just lie here sunbathing while they come to kill everyone?"

Crux cast him an angry look. "Just because I live in a cemetery, doesn't mean I'm eager to lie under one."

"He's scared," said Bridgette between sips, her wicked smile revealing a row of sharp teeth.

"No," Crux retorted, "I don't fear death. I'd just like to take my time getting there, that's all."

"What can I say to make you reconsider?" Jell asked.

"Show me a thousand baka on our doorstep."

Jell shook his head. "By that time it'll be too late." He noticed Henry was about to sample his drink. "Careful. Kleren is...hot."

Henry took a sip anyway. He wished he hadn't. The drink felt like liquid fire on his tongue, spices too hot for any mortal to handle. He spewed it across the table. Crux laughed and poured the remainder of his drink into his hand. Then, to Henry's amazement, he proceeded to wash his face with the spiced rum. Jell could see they weren't going to win this argument, so he thanked the Baron and his wife for their time.

After they had left, Henry turned to him, confused. "Does that guy really hold much influence here? He's insane."

With a finger to his lips, Jell cast him a wary glance. It was clear he didn't want to discuss anything until after they had left the cemetery. Only then did Henry notice the group of armed men resting in the shade of a nearby wall. Seeing that he and the Jellyman were indeed leaving, they slunk quietly back into the neighborhood.

* * *

As they walked away from the graveyard, Jell told Henry the story of Baron Crux. He was a survivor, one of many from the outer territories. When the baka attacked their cities, they'd narrowly escaped, fleeing across the desert plains. The Baron himself organized this exodus, leading his people through weeks of hardship in the wilderness. And now they were refugees in Ginen, forced to live in the only space available – the cemetery.

"They're accustomed to death," Jell said, not missing the irony. "I went to Crux first, because I knew it would make an impression. They aren't represented on the council."

"Why not?" Henry asked.

"The high priesthood argued against it."

"Well, it didn't sound like he was on our side either."

Jell frowned. "No, it didn't. And without his support, the Southern Cemetery won't join the fight. That would be quite a loss." He let the gravity of it sink in. "Crux answers to only one person - his wife. Let's hope we convinced her."

He glanced up at the sun to gauge the time. "Come on. We've much ground to cover." Henry had to jog now to match his pace. "Next we'll speak to the Marassas."

"Who are they?"

"Twins, each with power over a different quarter of the city. Though they look the same, their attitudes couldn't be more different. Jasmin lives to the west. She's wise beyond her years. Her sister, Iris, lives in the east. She's..." He trailed off, at a lost for words. "Twins don't get along," he said finally. "We must be careful."

They entered a neighborhood marked by high fences and locked gates, all somewhat reminiscent of Boca Raton, Henry thought. Bougainvillea crept over elegant walls, hiding shards of glass cemented at the top. Obviously, the residents here were concerned about security and had the wealth to afford it.

They finally arrived at a door cut into the side of a pruned cactus hedge that extended for almost a city block. Jell rapped twice on the wood in quick succession and then paused before adding a third knock. A burly man in fine satin opened the door and glowered down at them.

"State your business."

Jell leaned forward and whispered something into the guard's ear. Then without warning, he grabbed the man's hand in what Henry guessed was some kind of secret shake. The guard didn't look surprised at all by this; he simply stepped aside.

The interior could not have been more different from the Baron's house. It was like they'd stepped into another city. Mosaic floor tiles extended down an arched corridor, evenly lined with palmetto. Complex ironwork twisted to form the doors and windows. The décor reminded Henry of Miami's beachfront mansions.

"Nice gated community."

"This is the house of Jasmin Florentina," Jell said as they walked along the corridor.

"This is all one house? It looks like a museum." Henry paused to admire an Ibis sculpture resting in an alcove.

"She's very wealthy, as are many in the west."

"We just have good taste, that's all," whispered a nearby voice. Spinning around, they came face to face with a tall woman in her late thirties. An embroidered gown perfectly draped her elegant form, hugging her hips like an extension of the body.

"Jasmin, glad to find you home." Jell recovered quickly from the sight of her. "We've been looking forward to speaking with you."

"And I you. We were told you'd be coming."

"Then you must know the reason for my visit." Jell launched into the same detailed plea that he'd presented to Crux. After he'd finished, he waited patiently for Jasmin to digest his words. She bit her lip and then spoke very carefully.

"I understand what you're saying, and I agree...but we cannot win a war."

"Says who?" Jell asked.

Jasmin didn't answer. Her silence betrayed her thoughts.

"Someone's already spoken to you about this," Henry said. She smiled at his perceptiveness. Then she turned and rested a hand on Jell's shoulder.

"Sarn's in the courtyard with my sister. He arrived shortly before you did." Jell moved to pass her, but she'd anticipated this and blocked his path. "Wait, he's brought the city guard with him. I don't want trouble in my quarter, Jell." Her eyes underlined the seriousness in her voice.

"We won't cause any trouble. What did he tell you?"

"Only that you'd come and speak to us as you have. I told him I'd preferred to hear it from you, alone."

"And..."

"And..." Jasmin paused again, obviously still thinking, "I trust you Jelosquevo. I always have." She smiled softly. "You'll have the support of the Western Quarter to defend our city."

"I'm glad to hear that," Jell said.

"But my sister won't be so easily swayed. Sarn can be very convincing."

"So can I...," said Jell, striving past her towards a wide arch at the end of the corridor. They emerged upon a courtyard ringed by high balconies that spilled creeper vines into the patio below. At its center, a small group of men and women took refuge from the sun under a collection of umbrellas. Among those gathered, Henry immediately recognized the uniform of the city's guard and several members of the high priesthood. Sarn's skeletal form was difficult to miss. He sat on a bench next to a young woman who looked strikingly similar to Jasmin, but had lighter hair and a sterner expression.

"Ah," Sarn said, noticing their approach, "I see the Jellyman has finally decided to grace us with his presence. Seems he thought it more important to speak with the gravedigger first."

"Don't believe a word this man says, Iris. The baka will invade this city. We must prepare —"

"Why do you insist on spreading fear?" Sarn rose to his feet. "If the baka do invade, it will be because you've provoked them. Besides, we all know your true reason for taking arms." He leaned in close. "You want to return Riyal to power."

"This isn't about politics."

Sarn continued unabated, "Oh yes, it is. This has nothing to do with the baka. For everyone's safety, I'm placing you under arrest." He nodded to one of the guards. Henry's heart sank; he really didn't want to climb those tower stairs again.

"Let me speak my piece," Jell said with such force that the guard stopped in his tracks. "No matter what anyone does, in a few days all the forces of the baka will descend on this city. We can accept this and put up a strong fight, or we can roll over and let them kill us. Iris, please."

The young woman shook her head. "Jell, I think Sarn is right. The baka attacks are isolated. Those responsible for helping them have been killed. You're just disturbing the peace." Several guards moved in behind them, their hands on their sword hilts. The defeat in Jell's eyes was painful to witness. He looked over at Jasmin for support.

"I'm sorry. I can't make an enemy of the city guards," she whispered and stared down at her shoes.

"I think some time in the high tower will cool your fire." Sarn grinned with satisfaction. "Your head has swelled too much, little priest. Leave the governing of Ginen to the wise."

Hearing the approach of footsteps, Sarn looked across the courtyard. What he saw made his face drop. Baron Crux and a large contingent of his men were strolling across the tiles towards them.

"Put your little dick away, Sarn, and stop pissing on these good people."

"Baron Crux..."

"The Marassas won't have you. You're even uglier than I am. So stop wasting everyone's time, you old fart." Crux walked right up to Sarn and poked him in the chest with a thin finger. "No one wants to hear your long winded blabber."

Sarn glanced nervously at Crux's men. He was outnumbered now and knew he'd never win a fight. From the look of it, these men were itching for the chance.

"You're wise to heed my advice," Sarn said to Iris.

"What he means is that he wants to jump your bones." Crux started making thrusting motions in the air. Even some of the city guards chuckled at his. Sarn's face flushed red and his eyes shot daggers. But the Baron was only goaded on and began to grind himself against the high priest's leg. Sarn shook off the old man and turned to leave the courtyard in a huff. "Don't go, Sarn. Let us bask in your power,"

Crux said giddily. "At least he's treating us to views of his boney ass. How the women lust for those fine, wrinkled cheeks."

"You're vile," Jasmin said. Crux laughed as if she'd just paid him a great compliment.

"Good timing," Jell quickly interjected. "Thank you."

"Thank Sarn. If he's against you, you can count on the support of the Southern Cemetery." Crux gave a toothy grin. Jasmin nodded in turn and soon all eyes came to rest on Iris.

"I still think you're making a mistake," she said. "I can't tell my people to join you. I'm sorry." With that, she turned and followed Sarn out of the courtyard.

"Iris, wait," Jell tried to catch her, but she wouldn't listen.

"She'll come around," Jasmin assured them.

"I hope so." Jell watched her go with a worried look on his face. "We'll need the Eastern Quarter to defend Ginen." He turned back to Jasmin and Crux and began laying out his plans.

Henry wasn't listening, however. Instead, he stared intently at Jasmin's ears. A set of silver earrings hung from each lobe and twisted as she spoke. He made a mental note of their design, for he'd seen that veve in his picture book. This was likely the sign of her guardian angel, her "met tet", or whatever. Again, his gut told him this was important, but he couldn't understand why.

"Let's gather tonight at my peristyle," Jell said. "We can discuss the details then." They bid farewell to their new allies, left the tranquil estate for the bustling streets outside, and returned home. For much of the way, Henry remained silent, his mind lost in thought.

Chapter 19

Eyes had been on him for several days now, and Riyal knew it. He comforted himself in the knowledge that hope did not rest on his shoulders alone. Others were on his side now, and momentum was growing. Ginen would not be destroyed because of the corrupt laziness of a few. The seeds of hope had been planted. He stopped and broke away from his thoughts.

Where the hell am I?

Riyal didn't recognize the alley he'd been wandering down. He realized then how rarely he left the council ward, how little he interacted with the people he governed anymore. The night air had a chill to it, and the last thing he wanted was to get lost, so he stopped to orient himself. In the quiet of the alley, he heard footsteps on the cobblestones. They had been waiting for this moment.

Riyal brandished the walking staff he kept hidden beneath his cloak. He gestured towards the shadows.

"Come out. I know you're there."

The figures emerged slowly, men and women with cold, emotionless faces.

"You betray this city," he said to the gathering crowd. A dozen figures in dark robes now surrounded him. They blocked off any escape.

"Don't lecture us," one of them said. Riyal recognized the voice as that of the bald teacher who had served him breakfast that morning in Jell's study. "You've spoken enough," the teacher said.

But Riyal would not be so easily silenced. He stared the teacher down. "Do you think you're saving Ginen? Sacrificing the elderly, children —"

"We did what had to be done," one of them cryptically.

"You betray all of Ginen," Riyal yelled, his fist shaking in anger. "You betray your ancestors, you betray the lwa."

"It has nothing to do with the any of that," came a familiar voice. Riyal spun around, in shock. He was so stunned by who he saw that he couldn't speak. "This is about survival, Riyal. That's all. I'm sorry you can't see that."

Riyal recognized this man but couldn't believe it was really him. "You?...it can't be."

But the voice continued, "That expedition you sent could have started a war. It could have killed us all. But you're fortunate; we've taken measures against them."

Riyal finally found his voice and his eyes narrowed. "You can't cut a deal with the baka. The devil never keeps his promises."

"What choice do we have?"

Unexpectedly, Riyal smiled. "The lwa shall show us the way."

"After all this, you still believe?"

"Yes, I have hope," Riyal said.

"Hope is a dangerous thing."

"Only for the baka —" A swift blow to the back of the head interrupted his speech. Riyal collapsed to his knees as the attacker moved in for the kill.

"No, also for you, hope is a very dangerous thing," the man said.

The club came down with a sickening crunch.

Chapter 20

Gradually, the towers of Ginen shrunk to a speck on the horizon. The expedition party was now alone in the vast expanse of unspoiled dunes and water - although not quite alone. Carlos thought he saw someone off in the distance, watching them. A second figure materialized through the heat waves, followed by a dozen others. The dune ahead was soon crowded with them: tall, stationary figures looming dark against the sky. As the expedition party drew closer, however, Carlos saw that they were not people at all, but wooden columns sticking vertically out of the sand like telephone poles stripped of their wires. And there were thousands of them.

"The drift forest," Moro said. "We make camp there tonight."

They entered the forest of driftwood, hiking through a surreal landscape that Carlos realized must stretch for miles.

"Where does the wood come from?" he asked, prying at a salt-worn splinter.

"From the sea," Moro answered as if this was this were obvious. "The forest is home to angry lwa, the petra. The baka don't like to come here. So we should be safe." He lowered his voice. "But I hope they do come. I have a debt to settle."

"Killing them won't bring back her back."

"But we'll be even," Moro said, his eyes tearing up. Carlos wished Henry were here. His friend was an excellent grief counselor – a fact he knew from first hand experience.

"You should talk to Henry when we get back. He can help you work things out."

Ayzili scoffed and began rummaging through her pack. "Yes, and make you feel guilty for years."

"What've you got against him?"

"He's a priest. Need I a better reason?" She looked up from the pack, her dark hair whisking to one side.

"The Jellyman's a priest, and you're friends with him."

"That's different."

"How so?"

Ayzili scrunched up her eyes. She didn't have an answer, and Carlos knew he'd better change the subject. He suspected that Henry reminded Ayzili of her late husband, but he didn't dare ask for details. This was bottled up deep inside her. Best to leave those emotions alone.

Instead he remarked, "I noticed we didn't pack a tent, I mean a tapo. I'm guessing that's to make room for the poison. So, we just sleep out here in the open?"

"No, there's a place we use." After consulting a tiny compass, she pointed ahead through the timbers. "We must hurry, before the tide rises."

The group soon made their way to a section of the forest where the driftwood poles clustered together in tight formations. Carlos noticed a rusted dagger protruding from one of the timbers. He tried to remove it, but the metal disintegrated in his hands.

"This is where we camp," Moro said.

"Why here?" All Carlos saw was the endless forest of poles. With a mischievous grin, Ayzili grabbed his chin and tilted his head skyward. Carlos couldn't believe his eyes.

"What is that, a tree house?" An elaborate spider web of platforms and bridges hung above him, all built upon the towering driftwood.

"This used to be a village, before the baka came. Now it belongs to the dead," Moro explained. "This way." He motioned to a thick pole notched every few feet. The group had already begun ascending this crude ladder towards a wide platform and opened walled hut. Here, the men unloaded their packs.

"Welcome to the Village of Ghede," Moro said, once they'd re-assembled at the top. Carlos took a moment to take in his surroundings, a maze of derelict bridges and huts that stretched over at least three acres. From the rotting timbers, he guessed the village had been abandoned for some time. It would be a safe place to camp, at least from the baka. He turned his attention back to the group, wondering which of them was the traitor. Tonight he would check the sandals and be sure. "Watch your step. The tide's rising," Moro cautioned them.

"What did he mean by that?" Carlos asked Ayzili, as soon as he'd passed out of earshot. She pointed below. Following her gaze, he was shocked to see ocean waves already lapping at the base of the poles.

"Wow. That's fast."

"The tides are very powerful here. They'll keep us safe for the night."

"The lwa will keep us safe, not the waters," said a scruffy looking man with very few teeth.

"Like they did the villagers of this place?" Ayzili countered and the man fell silent. "Come," she said to Carlos. "I know the best place to lay our mats."

She led him across several bridges to a lone platform that commanded a wide view of the incoming tide. A thatched roof provided some cover and she hung a paper lantern by one of its rafters. Across the village, Carlos could see that others were doing the same. Throughout the village, misty halos of light began to emerge.

"Looks like a fog's moving in," he said.

"My grandfather called it the breath of the lwa."

"Then they've got halitosis," Carlos joked. Indeed, the fog was rolling in thick. Soon, they couldn't see beyond the bridge that connected their platform. Carlos had a strange sense of déjà vu. He's seen this before – the wooden pathway leading off to a small hut. It was exactly like the pier behind Mambo's grocery, the one that led to her secret storehouse. Has she been here? His stomach interrupted his thoughts.

"I'm famished," he said. "Want me to start dinner?"

"I'm going to sleep. Don't chew too loudly." Ayzili tossed him a hunk of cheese wrapped in cloth. Then she unfastened her sword, spread out her mat, and lay down. Soon her chest rose and fell with each breath, as she drifted off into rhythmic slumber.

"Ugh. This is terrible." Carlos gnawed on a corner of the cheese. He knocked it against a floorboard to show how hard it was. "I'm going to go see what other people are eating."

"Better hurry," she said sleepily. Carlos saw that the lights were fading out one by one through the mist.

"Don't wait up for me," he said, but she'd already fallen asleep. Carlos took a deep breath and slapped his face. He needed to be alert now. It was time to find out whose sandal matched the print he'd seen in the sand, the one that belonged to the spy.

* * *

Henry watched as Jell paced the school courtyard anxiously. Tonight they would know for sure how many of Ginen's quarters they could count as allies. Crux arrived first, although he brought less of an entourage than Henry suspected he might. The tall, skeletal man came accompanied by only three imposing men and his even more imposing wife, Bridgette. Catching Henry's eye, she smiled unexpectedly. He smiled back, but a shiver went up his spine as he did so. It's like flirting with a cadaver, he thought. The crowd soon increased, and Henry caught sight of Jasmin surrounded by a large gathering of men and women in elegant robes. Her sister, Iris, was not among them. Jell noticed her absence too, and it showed on his face. However, he couldn't wait any longer; it was time to get the meeting started.

"Thank you for biding my call tonight," he began and waited until the voices died down to a murmur. "You've heard my plea, so I will not belabor it. The threat is real. The baka have kept us alive as a cat plays with its prey. Now they mean to finish us off. The question is - how are we going to defend ourselves?"

"Our yamala resources are low," Jasmin said from across the courtyard.

"We've already dispatched an expedition to collect more. Once they return, we'll divide it equally amongst the quarters."

This earned a disgusted snort from Crux. "Who will decide what's equal?"

Before Jell could respond, he was interrupted by a commotion in the back of the crowd. A young member of his congregation pushed forward and rested his hand on a lemon tree to catch his breath.

"It's Riyal," he said.

"What about Riyal?" Jell asked with trepidation in his voice.

"The city guard found his staff and robes. They think he's been murdered."

"What? That can't be?" Jell staggered as if he'd been physically struck.

"His robes were soaked in blood."

Immediately the courtyard erupted into chaos as everyone started speaking at once. Accusations flew against the high priesthood and guards. Many people clamored for revenge. But Jell couldn't find his voice. He backed onto the bench next to Henry, his head cradled in his hands.

"He can't be dead."

Henry patted his shoulder. Until now, he never realized what Riyal meant to Jell. The large priest was acting like he'd just lost his father.

"He may still be alive," Henry said. Jell looked to the night sky as if the answers lay there.

"Without him, we are lost."

Henry had comforted many of his congregation during times of sorrow and knew the best thing to say was often nothing at all. So he remained silent and began unwrapping the strange gift that Riyal had given him. It appeared to be some type of bottle, thickly entwined in ribbon.

Jell looked over. "What are you doing?

"Unwrapping Riyal's gift."

"You don't unwrap a Congo packet. It'll loose its power." But it was too late; Henry let the last bit of ribbon fall to the side. What remained was a tiny glass bottle with a cork stopper. But that's not what caught Henry's eye. Inside the glass glinted a shiny object – a key.

"Hide it," Jell said immediately. "Show no one."

"He knew I'd unwrap this."

Jell nodded. Seeing the key had awoken him from his stupor. He stood up and walked to the center of the arguing crowd.

"People. Calm down. They want us to panic." His voice boomed throughout the courtyard. "There's no telling if Riyal is dead or alive. And we've no proof who might've harmed him." Henry was glad to see that Jell wasn't dwelling on Riyal's fate. They couldn't allow themselves to be paralyzed with fear. "We're at war," he continued, "and need to focus on what we can do now. There's not much time. First, we'll need a defense force..."

Crux pried himself off the wall and gave the crowd a crooked grin. "I'll handle that. I've seen my share of the battlefield. Send me your best men." His wife kicked him in the shins. "...and women. I can train them."

"We'll need weapons."

"We can provide that," Jasmin spoke firmly. "Our craftsmen will make the necessary spears and swords. But we'll need yamala. Without it, our weapons are useless."

"Then let us hope the expedition is successful." Jell scanned the room with renewed confidence.

Chapter 21

Mist drifted through the village like a parade of ghosts, streaming endlessly over the raised platforms and bridges. Below him, the tide had risen; timbers creaked and groaned with each ocean swell.

"I'm glad we didn't camp in the sand," Carlos whispered to himself. He took a deep breath and focused on his task. A spy had infiltrated their group, someone who was feeding the baka information, someone with access to restricted archives. If he could match their sandal to the footprint he'd seen there, he'd have proof.

Before long he came across a platform with three sleeping men. Although they appeared to be deep in slumber, they all kept their weapons within arm's reach. Carlos knew he'd have to tread cautiously here. He gingerly lifted the nearest sandal up by its leather straps. The sole was smooth – not a match. This could take a while, he realized. He quickly checked the other sandals, but none showed the radiating sun pattern, so he turned to leave. As he took the next step, however, the board beneath his foot creaked in protest.

He froze.

One of the men shifted in his sleep but did not wake. Carlos resumed breathing, moved off the platform, and hurried across the next bridge.

Soon he had checked over a dozen sandal pairs with no luck. The mist was thickening by the hour, and he began to fear he'd loose his bearings. The last thing he wanted was to get lost in this endless tree house. All he heard now was the ocean lapping at the poles beneath him and an occasional snore. A thin chill permeated the air. Salt spray stung his nostrils. The bridge beneath his feet trembled slightly, and Carlos stopped.

He wasn't sure if it was fatigue, but he swore he saw a figure's shadow ahead. A patch of fog momentarily obscured his vision, and then he saw the form again. Whoever it was must have seen him too. A dark shape fell from the bridge, plunging into the rolling waves with a splash. Carlos ran to the side and looked over. All he saw was the ebb and flow of the ocean and a few ripples.

Why would someone jump into that? Just to escape me? It didn't make any sense. He hadn't identified any sandals yet. But he had bent down and inspected that print in the sand, and now he was looking for matching soles. Someone could have seen him doing all this and put the pieces together. In fact, he felt like he was being watched this very second. Carlos spun around.

"You shouldn't be eating so late." Ayzili stood right behind him, wiping the sleep from her eyes. "What are you looking at down there?"

"I thought I saw someone jump," he said and then decided she deserved to know the whole story. He told her about the matching footprint, his theory about the spy, and the figure he'd just seen through the mist. Ayzili absorbed it all with a look of grave concern.

"I trust you," she said, "but many people have seen things in the Village of Ghede, things that don't exist."

"I still think we should gather everyone and see who's missing."

She gave him a long look as if weighing whether or not he was serious. Then she shrugged and cupped a hand to her mouth. The yell that she gave pierced his eardrums, but it had the desired effect. Soon the entire party had gathered back at the central platform where they'd first ascended. Most of the men had their weapons draw and were ready to fight.

"What's wrong?" they asked Ayzili.

"Who's missing?" She performed a quick headcount. "It's Moro. Anyone seen him?"

"He was sleeping alone in one of the outer huts." An older man pointed into the mist.

"He's no spy," Ayzili said, turning to Carlos. "He wouldn't help the baka after they killed his daughter."

"What's this about a spy?" one of the men asked.

Carlos sighed. "We believe there's a spy in our midst, someone with connections to the high priesthood and probably the baka."

A tall man spoke up from the back of the group. "If Moro's in league with the baka, it would explain why he left his daughter home without protection."

Carlos shook his head. Only a real monster would sacrifice his daughter. Moro's pain had felt real, his anger genuine. But the theory did fit the facts.

"Everyone remove your sandals," Ayzili said, kicking off her own. The look in her eyes was reason enough for the others to comply. "Look at them," she said. "Tell me if there's a match."

Grabbing a nearby lantern, Carlos made his way down the row of discarded sandals. None matched the print he had seen in the sand earlier that day.

"It was Moro," Ayzili said, "and I believed his act."

Carlos still wasn't convinced. "Someone could have two pairs of sandals."

"Only you would bring extra weight along," Ayzili said. "These men know better." She let out a long sigh. "It was Moro. He knew you suspected him, and he fled."

"We need more evidence," Carlos cautioned her.

"Your ways mean nothing here. If Moro's a spy, I hope he drowns swimming to higher ground." She turned angrily and marched back across the bridge towards her sleeping platform.

* * *

They both guessed what the key unlocked – the archives. Riyal wanted them to them to find something there, something he couldn't. And he knew his life was in danger. That's why he'd passed the task onto them. The only question was how to get into the gardens without drawing suspicion. With the Council disbarred, the priests were the only ones who could grant them access, so they needed an excuse. However, by the time he and Jell had reached the entrance, Henry still hadn't thought of a convincing one.

A junior priest stood guard beneath the giant door to the gardens. Torchlight illuminated his slouched form as he read from a scroll. Here goes nothing, thought Henry.

"Young man," Jell called out.

"Who's there?"

"Jelosquevo of the Northern Quarter." The young priest gave them a long stare. He didn't recognize Jell, which meant he was not tainted by Sarn's views - a stroke of luck.

"What's your business?" he asked.

"We're delivering reports from the palace guard."

"I wasn't told..." The young man's eyes narrowed. "I'll need to confirm this." Jell tried to respond but faltered. So Henry stepped in.

"This is business Sarn wants to keep secret," he whispered. Henry put his arm around the young priest's shoulders. "It's a delicate topic. And if you go announcing it to the whole hermitage, he's going to be none too pleased. You don't want to see him like that."

"I know," the young man said, evidently from experience.

"Now, he's on edge as is with all that's been going on. Let's do this one by the book and not cause a stir."

"Right, by the book." It was evident the young man didn't know what this meant, but Henry said it with such authority that he went to the door and started turning the latches. The huge doors swung open with their dramatic grinding noises.

"Don't tell him I gave you any trouble," the young man said.

"We won't. You did it by the book. Thanks." And just like that, they were inside the garden.

"That was impressive," Jell said as they snuck past the statues that guarded the entrance.

Henry smiled. "People are just like locks - you have to know which buttons to push to get them to open up."

His smile soon vanished, however, as he surveyed the gardens. The awe he'd first experienced was gone. After all, people had died here. The air felt heavy, the shadows menacing. A thin mist rose above from the stream and swirled about the mango trees. This place holds many more secrets, Henry thought, dangerous secrets. We're not safe here.

"How'd you know he'd react that way to hearing Sarn's name?" Jell asked.

"Fear can easily blind your judgment." Henry replied and then lapsed into silence. The guard wasn't the only one scared right now.

They walked along the edge of the waterfall pool where the priests had recently constructed a grate. It shimmered just beneath the surface, strangely alien amidst all the natural beauty. Henry's foot throbbed with pain as if to remind him of what had happened here. Moving quickly on, they ducked through the orchard and arrived at the archive.

A blast of cold air greeted them, rustling Jell's gown. His eyes grew wide in anticipation, and he rubbed his hands together eagerly. This was a moment Jell had been waiting years for, Henry realized.

He hoped it lived up to his expectations. Without speaking, he slid Riyal's key into the lock. It turned easily, the bolt slid to one side, and the gate swung outward with a creak.

"You think anyone's inside?" Henry asked, checking the ground for footprints. He saw many, but a thin layer of dust coated them all.

"Not this late." Jell gave Henry a sideways glance. "But I've never been inside before, only priests."

"And Riyal."

Jell nodded in respect. "When he was alive."

"We don't know —"

"Yes, we do," Jell said. "He's gone to the deep waters."

The corridor dropped into darkness and as it did, Jell produced a small torch from his pack. With a sharp movement against flint, he had it lit. The flames illuminated a corridor carved with intricate designs.

"I've seen these symbols before," Henry whispered, "What did you call them?"

"Veves...for the lwa. It's said they built these halls."

"You believe that?"

"I keep an open mind," Jell said.

The phrase reminded Henry of something he'd once said back in Miami. He'd suggested to Carlos that he pray for his daughter. When Carlos asked him if he thought that would really help, he'd replied the same way Jell had. He told him to keep an open mind.

Jell gave him an odd look, likely wondering why Henry had lapsed into silence. Then he shrugged and continued forward down the tunnel. The corridor soon widened into a circular room with a central column as thick as a Redwood.

"It looks like your temple."

"Yes, it's a peristyle. But where are the scrolls? There are supposed to be scrolls." Instead, the walls overflowed with carvings, hundreds of them. Amongst these designs, a number of statues peered out from their wall alcoves, each representing a certain spirit, Henry guessed.

"Hey this guy's a dead ringer for Crux," he said, wincing at the unintended pun. Before Henry stood the statue of a tall, cadaverous man in a top hat, the eyes vacant and sunken.

"That's Baron Samedi, lwa of death. He's Crux's met tet."

"Ahhh. Guardian angle. But why is he smiling?"

"Because he's a jokester."

"Riyal's the real jokester," Henry said. "There's nothing here —"

"Shhh..." Jell raised his hand.

"What is it?" And then he heard it too - the creak of the gate opening, followed by voices growing in volume. People were headed their way. Henry looked at the statues, too small to hide behind. And the column wouldn't provide much cover if it were a large group. They were trapped.

Then something occurred to him.

Jell said that spirits built these archives. I'll bet the original architects wanted to perpetuate that myth, Henry thought. So they built the entrance in a way that spirits would use. So how would spirits enter an archive?

"You said the lwa join you during your ceremonies? They come to your peri —

"Peristyle...yes from the deep sea." Jell pushed him behind the center column, out of view of the corridor. Soon they would have to extinguish their torch.

"How exactly do they travel to you?"

"The lwa? They enter through the poto mitan. Through this!" he slammed his first against the column and was greeted by a dull hollow sound. The noise reverberated like a stone dropped down an elevator shaft. They both looked at each other.

"There's got to be a door," Henry whispered.

They could hear voices down the corridor without straining now. Soon they'd be discovered. Circling the column, Henry pressed on every protruding carving he could find. No, it won't be random, he thought.

St. Peter guarded the entrance to Heaven. What is his counterpart here? Mentally, Henry flipped back the pages of the book Jell had given him. Oh, yes....the crippled old man. Papa something. He saw the statue tucked away in a far alcove - an old man leaning on a crutch. The staff moved as he pressed against it. He heard the grind of gears and then a sharp click as the creases of a door broke away from the pillar behind him.

"I've found it."

Jell thrust his torch through the secret doorway. The column was indeed hollow, and its shaft didn't end at the floor. It sank precipitously down an endless well. No stairs, just a steep drop into blackness. Footsteps echoed behind them.

"Push off the wall," Henry said and jimmied into the shaft. By pressing against its side with his back and good foot he could suspend himself from falling. He crawled a little higher to allow Jell inside.

"This is a bad idea," Jell said before shutting the door and following Henry's lead of pressing against the sides. The door snapped shut behind him and just in time - the muffled voices had arrived outside. Henry held his breath.

"...was no choice. I know."

Henry didn't recognize the speaker's voice. It was still too far away. He heard heavy breathing and glanced down. Jell was struggling to support his weight; beads of sweat dotted his brow and his face flushed with the strain of keeping still. Henry was having difficulty himself. He tried to shift his weight to the other foot, but the wound prevented it. Pain shot up his joints. More voices chimed in from outside the column. This was a large gathering.

"I saw Riyal lurking around here. He must've known of our meetings," came a loud booming voice.

A lighter, whining voice, followed this. "I told you we shouldn't have met here."

"The ghost stories kept most away, didn't they?"

Tiny legs crawled across his arm. Henry looked over to see a white cave spider inching up his bicep. Then he felt something strike his head and he whisked off another insect. The smoke from the torch must be dropping them from the ceiling. He saw that Jell struggled now just to hold the flame. The voices outside continued...

"It wasn't us, he was after."

"Then what was it?"

"I don't know. The old man was crazy. Thought the archives would save us all."

"He had many foolish ideas. And his death only bought us time. Others will take up his cause. We need to send another envoy to the baka. They're getting anxious."

A shuffling sound echoed up from below. Jell's knees shook from the effort of keeping himself aloft. He wouldn't be able to hold out much longer. But Henry knew they couldn't leave now. If these were the same people who killed Riyal, they were in grave danger. He just hoped their gathering would be a short one. His own leg was beginning to shake.

"They didn't respond very well to the last envoy."

"Zui wasn't the best choice. He hardly knew the language."

"I hope he tasted good, at least."

"Shut up," came a female voice. This one, Henry thought he recognized. It sounded like Iris, one of the Marassa twins. He looked down at Jell and his face confirmed it. "Don't make light of our situation," she continued. "I'll meet with the baka. I can speak the language well enough. A new pact must be formed."

"That won't be easy. With the waterfall sealed, we have nothing to bargain."

"No, there will soon be another way into the city."

A slight groan escaped Jell's lips. His face had turned crimson, his whole body now shaking. He looked up at Henry and, tightening his jaw, handed over the torch. Henry grabbed it and then held out his free hand, but Jell refused. He wouldn't take them both down. Without saying a word, he let go and fell silently away into the shadows. Henry never heard him connect with the ground. It must've been quite a distance. Nausea twisted his stomach.

Then he felt a sharp pain at his wrist – a spider.

Henry flinched and began to slide loose. Scrambling to find a hold, he realized he'd exhausted his strength. His fingernails scratched at the air, and he tumbled backwards into a free fall. The light vanished. Darkness closed in...

Chapter 22

Henry opened his eyes. A galaxy of stars glittered overhead, however, the air still retained a musty, subterranean smell. *How is this possible?*

"They're not stars." Jell had his neck craned to the heavens. He turned back and helped Henry to sit up.

"Where are we?"

"Look at this." Jell opened his hand to reveal a fat grub twisting about his palm. Organs inside its belly glowed a brilliant green, like a ghostly egg roll.

"Glowworms?" Henry asked.

"Yes, the ceiling's covered in thousands of them."

As Henry's eyes adjusted to the darkness, he saw that he lay in a cavernous chamber, the ceiling of which sparkled with constellations. This eerie light illuminated a sloping tunnel, like a dried out water slide, which curved out from the wall and into the pit where they currently sat. *The sand here must have cushioned our landing,* Henry thought. *Riyal could have warned us about this.* He checked his head for signs of injury but found no bumps. So Henry turned his attention to the rest of the cavern.

Rows of wooden scaffolding stretched ahead of him, dispersed amongst the stalagmite knobs. What appeared to be paper towel rolls threaded the length of the racks. No, they were scrolls, thousands of scrolls, cracked and yellowed with age. And that wasn't all. Bookshelves, filled with thick tomes and reams of parchment, lined the outer walls. Everywhere Henry looked he saw paper and ink, a vast library bathed in eerie green light - the archives.

"This is what Riyal wanted us to find," he said.

"Yes," Jell sat back on a rock and stared at him strangely. "I'm hungry. Do you have any chicken? I really do love those tasty birds."

Jell was babbling nonsense. He must have hit his head on the way down. Henry looked the priest over, but he seemed unscathed: no blood or bruises; no lumps on his head. Maybe he was just in shock. "You have the food, remember?"

Rummaging through his pack, Jell smiled. "Ah, my horse brought it. But no chicken. Pity." He removed a mango and began to cut into the fleshy pulp with a knife.

"Your horse? What are you talking about?" Henry suddenly felt very alone. This was the worst place for Jell to loose his mind - stranded underground with little food or water. They needed to find a way back to the surface.

But Jell seemed unconcerned with their predicament. "The Jellyman, I should have known he'd bring food. He's never without it."

Henry stood up slowly. Why is Jell talking about himself in the third person? "Who am I talking to?" he asked.

"Azaka," Jell said, smiling.

Henry decided to humor him. "Are you a spirit?"

Jell nodded and then tossed a slice of mango into his mouth. Great. Jell thinks he's possessed. Henry groaned and pinched the bridge of his nose.

"Why don't you rest, Mr. Zaka? I'll look around for an exit."

Jell smiled knowingly, as if sensing Henry's disbelief. "The way out is right over there." Henry followed his outstretched hand to a door at the opposite end of the cavern. It stood ajar, framing a staircase that spiraled upward and out of view.

"Do you mind if I test it?" Jell simply shrugged. So Henry added, "It's not that I don't trust you." It's just that you've lost your bloody mind, he thought to himself as he jogged through the scroll racks.

The stairwell spun upward for a few twists, before emptying into a hall. At its end, Henry came across a ladder that led to the ceiling. He guessed there was a trapdoor here and pressed his ear against the flagstone. Voices drifted through the rock, but they were muffled and unintelligible. This must lead to the hallway of statues where they'd first entered. Escape was unthinkable until the meeting adjourned, so he returned to Jell in the archive.

"We'll have to wait."

"Why do you want to leave?" Jell asked, his mouth full of mango. "The answers are all here."

Riyal's words came back to Henry as he scanned the rows of parchment.

The way to save Ginen lies within the archive.

Maybe some ancient text here explains how to deal with the baka, exposes a weakness? He wished Jell wasn't delirious. The task before him would challenge a team of academics, let alone one person. Well, he was a religious scholar in an ancient archive; it was clear what he had to do.

* * *

The sun rose a violent red over the horizon of driftwood poles. Carlos lifted his head from the mat and took in the scent of dried fibers and salt. The first thing he saw was Ayzili, gnawing on a bit of dried meat.

"Moro hasn't returned," she said, tilting her head. "Maybe he drowned."

"We should search for him."

Even if he were dead, his body might tell them something. Carlos didn't like loose ends, and Moro's disappearance certainly qualified as one. But Ayzili wasn't going to spare another minute on a man she considered a traitor.

"We don't have time. We've got to continue the harvest. Eat up, we move out within the hour."

They continued on through the driftwood forest until the poles began to thin out and then disappear all together. The beachhead curved close here, and the sound of waves filled their ears.

"We should have seen a fresh crop by now," one of the taller men said. He ran a hand across his sweaty mane and then, with a grunt of frustration, threw his pack into the sand. The group came to a halt at the base of a large dune, its towering height hiding the coastline from view. "We should return and help defend Ginen."

The other men also heaved their packs into the sand and collapsed next to them. Canteens were unfastened and passed around.

The taller man continued his rant. "No wonder we've had such bad luck. Moro misled us. There's likely no yamala for miles." From the silence that followed this statement Carlos knew many were thinking the same thing.

But Ayzili hadn't even taken off her pack. "We can't return empty handed," she said evenly. "There's not enough yamala to defend Ginen."

"At least we can fight," the tall man said as he patted the sword sheathed at his side. "Instead of returning to a city in ruins."

Ayzili walked over to the man and started arguing vehemently. But Carlos's attention was drawn elsewhere, to another sand dollar that lay at his feet. Something wasn't right. There were footprints underneath the shell, and yet it wasn't cracked or damaged in any way. That meant it was dropped recently.

He reached down and snatched the shell up. Turning it over, he saw that someone had scratched a crude map onto the back. The etched lines clearly showed the coastline, driftwood forest, and their current path. Instantly, he realized the implications; not only was the spy still alive, but he was actively leaking their location through these dead drops. Carlos quickly scanned the group, hoping to catch someone looking at him. But no one seemed concerned that he held the shell. Ayzili's argument with the longhaired man still captured most of their attention.

"We still have time," she said, her face red with anger.

"No we don't, and you know it." The man stamped the ground repeatedly. "We must return." Carlos noticed that his feet were red with blisters. Pain guided his words. But that was not all he noticed – the man's sandals didn't fit. They were too small.

They weren't his.

Rising to his feet, Carlos brandished the sword Ayzili had given him. He pointed it at the tall man.

"He's wearing Moro's sandals."

"What?"

The man yanked his sword from the sheath. Before he could raise it, however, Ayzili had knocked the weapon from his hand with a swift kick. The blade sliced into the sand several feet away.

"You killed Moro, didn't you? And for what?" Carlos asked, shaking his head sadly. "Just to throw us off track?" This was a premeditated murder - he'd killed in cold-blood just to shift the attention from himself, to frame Moro as the spy. It made Carlos sick. He looked over the traitor, sizing him up. Well over six feet tall, he bore a puffy face as if his cheeks were stuffed with food. Long hair fell to his shoulders, and he stared through the strands with a stern, unblinking visage.

"You think you're so clever," the man said. His voice turned icy, laced with disgust.

"Who is this?" Ayzili asked. By now, everyone had drawn weapons.

"He's a friend of my cousin's," said a man carrying a long spear. "His name is Trey."

"Can anyone vouch for his loyalty?" Ayzili already knew the answer to her question and wasn't surprised when no one spoke up.

Carlos locked eyes with Trey. But the man showed no fear at having been discovered – quite the opposite in fact. He appeared to relish the confrontation. "You saw that I was trying to match a sandal pattern, didn't you?" Carlos asked.

"You think you're saving everyone, but you're only hastening death."

Trey's head snapped back, and he fell to the sand. Ayzili shook the fist that she'd hit him with and cursed.

"Did you kill Moro?" she screamed.

Trey wiped the blood from his mouth and spit into the sand. "I did what I had to."

His voice wavered slightly, and Carlos picked up on it. There was a hint of fear. Now was their chance.

"We know you're not the mastermind," he said gently. "Give us names and I'll guarantee your safety."

Trey seemed to weigh this for a second, but then he shook his head. "I don't think so..." From behind his back, he removed a small conch shell with a hole at one end. He raised it to his lips and blew a long note that the wind carried aloft. One of the other men ripped the shell away, but it was too late.

High on the dune, a dark shape skittered into view. Many others joined it, until the silhouettes of dozens of baka filled the horizon. Trey's mouth curved into a sick smile.

"Now you see who controls the power in Ginen. Not the elders, the priests, or the guards. It's us, those who've allied with the baka. We decide who lives or —" Ayzili kicked him squarely in the jaw before he could finish.

"Fall back," she screamed. "Get to higher ground."

The sand below them started to vibrate with the pounding of dozens of crab legs. Like a stampede of wild horses, the baka moved down the slope with alarming speed, their claws outstretched and snapping. The designs on their shells gleamed in the sun, elaborate crisscrossing red spirals, Celtic looking. As they approached, several baka let out a chattering war cry.

One of the men let loose a volley of arrows, which clattered harmlessly against the nearest shell.

"Wait until they're closer," Ayzili yelled back and sprinted up the nearest dune. Carlos followed close behind her.

"You won't have to wait long," he said. "Hurry!" Soon the baka were right on top of them. The creatures rushed past Trey without giving him a sideways glance and charged up the incline.

"Now," Ayzili screamed. "Take them out." She reached into the folds of her shirt and palmed a marble. Without hesitation, she flung it at the nearest baka, shattering poison across its front in a rain of shards. The creature reeled up on its hindquarters and toppled backwards into the sand, its legs curled into a death embrace. Other members of the party followed Ayzili's lead, flinging their orbs or shooting arrows into the oncoming fury. Most hit their mark and the first wave of baka fell back. But one of the older men had aimed too high and missed his target. The baka in front of him thrust out its pincer and severed the man's head with a quick slice. His lifeless body fell to the sand like a discarded rag doll.

Carlos stared on in shock. He had seen people die before, but not like this. He felt a sharp pain across his face. Ayzili had slapped him.

"Wake up. We need higher ground."

The next wave of baka had already started up the dune. Ayzili handed Carlos a few marbles. "Aim with care," she said and ran towards the crest. The expedition party retreated behind her, and Carlos felt his calves burn as he hurried up the loose sand. The ground tremors were coming quicker now, and he saw that the baka had picked up speed. These creatures were far more maneuverable in this environment, their legs churning the sand like thoroughbreds. Why has Ayzili led them up the slope? She read his concern.

"Calm yourself," she said as she reached over her shoulder and drew her bow. Carlos hadn't even noticed that she was wearing one. In a quick succession, she let fly three arrows. They connected squarely with the mouth of the nearest baka. The force sent it toppling backwards, knocking over several others in the process. The confusion slowed their advance considerably. Ayzili smiled mischievously. Then her eyes widened. A shadow crossed the sand and she stepped backwards.

Carlos spun around to face a towering blue shell. He had never seen a baka like this – an alien form of purple blotches stretched over a thick bumpy surface. The pincer came down fast, but he ducked in time, and it sliced deep into the sand behind him. Carlos rolled out from under the claw and clutched one of the marbles tightly. But the creature was too close, and he knew shattering any of the orbs now would likely doom him as well. Another pincer flew through the air. Carlos barely sidestepped it. The creature pulled back and reeled up on its hind legs for a final attack. As it did, several of Ayzili's arrows connected with a soft patch beneath its belly. The baka let out an ear-piercing scream before rolling backwards into the swarming mass. Dozens more jockeyed to take its place.

Everywhere now, the baka fought in close quarters with the expedition members. Screams filled the air, but Carlos didn't have time to look. He followed the lithe form of Ayzili up the dune towards a crest that never seemed to get any closer. Out of the corner of his eye, he saw a man fall to the sand in a spray of blood. The baka descended on him and tore his limbs apart. The sight of blood seemed to drive them wild.

Carlos saw a young boy, no older than eighteen, cowering beneath a baka's claw. Without thinking, he flung a marble over the young man's head – straight down the creature's gullet. It took a second for the poison to work, but the baka stumbled and then collapsed into the dust. A smaller crab crawled over the fallen carcass and pounced on the teen, but the boy kicked it off and ran towards them up the dune.

Ayzili tugged on Carlos's arm. "Keep going to the top."

He pulled back. "They're being slaughtered."

"And so will you." She yanked his arm so hard, he thought it might pull from the socket. Carlos relented. He tried to ignore the screams as he followed Ayzili to the crest of the dune. Not until they'd reached it did he look back. The dune below was littered with the bodies of expedition members, mangled and trampled by the advancing baka horde.

"They've wiped out half of us," he whispered.

"And for that, they'll suffer." Ayzili dumped the contents of her quiver into the sand, thin arrows sliding out like a pack of spaghetti. She emptied a tiny sac of marbles next to it. Carlos noticed that all the men who'd made it this high were doing the same. Only a dozen or so of them remained, forming a ring around the top of the dune. The creatures paused their advance, wary as to why the attacks had momentarily halted. An especially large quartermaster jerked up from the body it had been feasting on, its face smeared with blood.

"This is for Sasha," Ayzili said and let go of the bow's string. The arrow whistled through the air and sunk into the baka with such force, it skewered through to the back shell, echoing a resounding crack as it connected. Before the creature had fallen to the sand, however, Ayzili had threaded a new arrow and let fly. "This is for Hungar."

Her eyes darted across the dune's face, searching out target after target. Soon a rain of death descended upon the baka. Arrow after arrow spiraled into the creatures, the poisoned tips always finding their mark. Carlos grabbed a fist full of marbles and heaved them one at a time into the fray.

Finally he understood why Ayzili had led them up here. From this vantage point, they could strike any of the creatures. And as the dead fell away, they left the ones behind exposed. Carlos easily picked off the crabs one after another, their legs curling backwards, shells crashing hard to the sand. Everywhere below them now, baka coiled up and screamed. The air rang thick with their cries. And then the tide shifted. The horde began to back down.

"Don't let them out of range." Ayzili leapt from her position and raced down the slope. She mounted the shell of a retreating baka and thrust her sword into a crack between its joints. Prying open the seam, she stabbed the underlying meat with her ankle dagger and rolled off. The baka tripped and stumbled in a spiraling cloud of dust. Through the swirling particles, Carlos caught a glimpse of Ayzili, sword in hand. She looked mythical - slashing at the claws that barely missed her, the beads in her hair swinging round in a complex dance. And then the dust settled. Dozens of the creatures lay dead in the wake of the expedition's charge. The remaining baka retreated across the valley and out of sight. The battle had been won.

Now a deathly silence washed over the group. Carlos could barely fathom that he was still alive. It reminded him of the drug cartel busts in Miami – extreme violence followed by surreal disbelief. He scanned for Ayzili and found her crouched over her sword, exhausted and drenched in dust.

"How many? she asked.

"Survivors, you mean? I count only ten."

"That bastard. Did he survive?" It took Carlos a second to register whom she was referring to. In the confusion of battle, he'd forgotten about Trey, the spy who'd launched the ambush.

"There's no sign of him," one of the men answered.

"Good," Ayzili said. "I've had enough killing for today." She sheathed her sword and rose to her feet. "Let's bury the fallen quickly...before the baka return and slaughter the rest of us."

Chapter 23

The scroll crackled as Henry unrolled it. He was half afraid the brittle parchment might disintegrate in his hands. Elaborate script and drawings shimmered in Jell's torchlight. He peered closer at the text.

Aequam memento rebus in arduis servare mentem.

"The language of the ancients," Jell said, peering over his shoulder.

"It's Latin!" Henry couldn't believe it. He adjusted his spectacles and started to translate. "Remember to keep an even mind in difficult situations."

That sounded familiar. Then he remembered the source. "Horus, the Roman poet. Incredible." He reached for another scroll and discovered a series of numerals; the next one had more text. The entire rack appeared filled with Roman documents. He let out a sigh. It'd been a while since his language courses in Seminary.

"Do you speak Latin?" he asked Jell.

"No, but my horse does."

More possession nonsense. Jell's condition hadn't improved much. At least he's imagined a friendly spirit, Henry thought. Then he shook his head. "How can something that posses you be friendly?" Speaking louder, he added, "I could use your help....there's a lot to search through around here."

That was an understatement. They faced an immense amount of information. It felt like he was drafting a sermon, overwhelmed with options. How long had that old man Riyal spent searching for the answers? Years, maybe. Jell watched as he shuffled from rack to rack.

"The answers you seek are not hidden," Jell said. "They lie in plain sight."

Henry blew out an exasperated breath, hiding his anger behind the scrolls. "Well, could you give me a hint?" How long was Jell going to continue speaking in riddles? He'd just about had enough of this. Stepping out from behind the rack, Henry threw his hands in the air. "Look, I think it's high time you dropped this act and helped out a bit here."

In response to his outburst, Jell simply grinned. Then his eyes rolled to the ceiling, legs buckled, and his whole body went limp. Henry hurried to catch him before his head hit the floor.

"Where are we?" Jell asked, blinking as if he'd just woken from a nap.

"The archives. Watch your step there, Azaka."

Jell gazed around the room in amazement. "How long have we been here?"

"A few hours. You should rest..."

Jell's face flashed excitement. "Why did you call me Azaka? Was I taken by the lwa?" His entire demeanor had changed, which Henry took as a good sign. He'd finally realized this whole possession charade was a huge waste of time.

"Who am I talking to now?" Henry asked, dryly.

"It's me, Jell."

"Well, thank God. That Zaka fellow was useless."

What did he say?" Jell asked, ignoring Henry's sarcasm. He rose to his feet and rubbed his head.

"Honestly, you weren't too helpful."

"Did he mention anything about the baka?"

"No, all you did was lecture me and then faint," Henry said.

"Azaka should have helped us." Jell sighed. But his disappointment was soon replaced by awe as he took in his surroundings.

Henry shrugged. "Perhaps you should ask the Lord for guidance, instead of all these spirits."

"The Lord is not my met tet," Jell said, referencing his guardian angel.

"Maybe he should be. Look at where these spirits have led Iris. She's sacrificing children to them."

Immediately, Henry knew he had gone to far. Jell cleared his throat and laid a heavy stare on him. "None of the lwa I serve would demand the sacrifice of a child. That is murder."

Henry raised his hands, afraid Jell might strike him. "I didn't mean any offense."

Jell rose to his full height, his voice booming. "The people who've allied themselves with the baka are evil." He placed a firm grip on Henry's shoulder. "They don't serve the spirits, they've abandoned them. Most lwa protect children."

"Ok," Henry said, not wanting to upset Jell anymore. His grip felt like a vice.

"The lwa speak through us. That is an honor. They impart their wisdom. And our world is better for it."

Oh come on, Henry thought. First you pretend a spirit possesses you, and then you get angry when you're called out on it. He had to admit the performance was convincing. But Henry wasn't about to forgive Jell's theatrics. Does he really think this is going to make a convert out of me?

Thankfully, Jell relaxed his grip and steered the conversation away from theology, saying, "Iris doesn't believe in the lwa. The only reason she listened to Sarn was because it fit with her plan to buy time. The high priests advocate doing nothing."

"Which would give her and the others time to renegotiate with the baka," Henry thought aloud, "guaranteeing their safety for a new route into the city."

"You heard that too, eh?" Jell said. "We must hurry then." He glanced at the racks, stretching far across the room. "The answers Riyal sought are here somewhere."

"By all means. I've been looking for a while." Henry collapsed onto a wooden bench. Don't tell me to hurry, he thought. You're the one wasting time being possessed.

Jell scratched his beard. “If Riyal couldn’t find it, the text must be well hidden.”

“Like the entrance to this place,” Henry said absently. Puzzles within puzzles. What had Jell said when he was acting possessed? The answer lay within plain sight. Maybe there’s something to that...

* * *

After the expedition party buried their fallen, several of the men began to recite prayers. Ayzili, however, was already on the move. She walked up the next dune and stopped at its crest. Carlos hurried to her side, where he noticed that she was holding her breath.

“What is it? he asked. She turned to look at him, and her shocked expression melted into a tight smile. Carlos followed her nod out towards the coastline. He gasped. Hundreds, thousands of dark shapes filled the tide pools. It would take an army to fight this many baka. But the dark shapes weren’t moving. Looking closer, he saw that they weren’t crabs at all...

“They’re blowfish,” Carlos said out loud. He recognized the spiky creatures from the tanks at his daughter’s favorite restaurant. She used to tap on the glass, spooking the fish so they’d inflate twice their normal size. But those had been no bigger than a grapefruit. The blowfish littering the ground before him were the size of weather balloons. Thousands of the huge creatures lay washed up and dead in the gentle surf.

“That’s a good crop. That’s what that is.” Several of the other men came up behind them. Many shouted for joy.

“I’ve never seen that many before.”

"It's a miracle."

Ayzili bit her lip. "We've got work to do."

As they approached the nearest fish, a powerful stench assaulted their noses.

Carlos gagged. "Aw. That's awful."

The animals were bloated - flesh rotting, eyes bulging, and spiked bellies extended to the bursting point.

"You think that's bad?" Ayzili drew her sword and poked the blade gently into the fish's stomach. With a loud hissing noise, the body deflated in a swirling cloud of green gas.

"Oh God." Carlos bent over and sacrificed his lunch to the sand. He felt Ayzili's hand on his back, patting him gently. Her touch sent a shiver up his spine, something he hadn't felt in quite a while. As several of the other men approached, she withdrew.

"Watch. You don't want to miss this," she said.

One of the men unrolled a leather bound kit on the sand. The instruments nestled inside resembled dental picks and gleamed viciously in the sun. He knelt before the deflated carcass and cracked his knuckles.

"It's a delicate process. One wrong move —"

"And what?" Carlos asked, feeling slightly better.

"Yamala everywhere," the man said, raising what looked like a scalpel. He made an explosion gesture with his free hand.

"Poison?" Carlos asked. Ayzili nodded. "Then how do you extract it?"

"Just watch," she said.

The man made a Y-shaped incision beneath the fish's eye. Using a set of tweezers, he pulled back the skin to reveal a tangle of organs underneath.

"The fish has eleven deadly parts," the man explained. "The liver has the most poison."

"The ovaries do," Ayzili corrected him.

"But those are sacred," the man said. "We don't harvest those." Ayzili rolled her eyes and bit her lip. The man pinned back the skin flap and set to work making a series of tiny incisions. As he severed each sinew, it shrunk away like an elaborate clock mechanism. Peeling back, they revealed an opaque organ drenched a deep burgundy from the poison. The man put away his knife and pulled on a set of leather gloves. Carefully, he reached into the bowels of the fish and removed the organ.

"This could kill a quarter of Ginen," he said, gingerly hefting it for weight. He set the liver down gently in a wax-lined box. Securing the lid, he lit a candle and let the wax drip along the outer seal. Then he pooled a glob of wax on top and pressed his ring into it. One of the other younger survivors came running up to them. Carlos recognized him as the young boy whose life he had saved on the dunes.

"What is it?" Ayzili asked.

"A lot of the fish have scuff marks. It looks like they were dragged here."

"No wonder that traitor wanted the party to turn around," Ayzili said. "He knew where the baka were stashing the crop."

"Not the baka," Carlos said slowly. "Notice these footprints? They're not ours." He crouched before the indentations in the sand. "...And here. Drag marks showing where rope's been used." It instantly became clear to everyone the extent of the conspiracy against them. It was not the baka, but people from Ginen, who had deliberately hidden this poison supply.

"They threw their lot in with the devils." Ayzili spat angrily. "Well, we've found their stash. Let's collect it all."

"Ayzili, we've lost fourteen," the man with the poison box said. "We can only carry so much back this trip."

She wouldn't listen. "We don't have time for another. We have to harvest as much as we can."

"The baka will be waiting in ambush," the teen said. "Maybe we should go back through the dunes."

"No, time is running out." Ayzili looked into the faces of the survivors. Her features hardened. "If we don't get back soon, it may be too late."

"What about the ocean?" Carlos asked. He got only silence in response. Everyone turned to look at him in disbelief. "Why don't we sail back? Can the baka swim out very far?" The men shook their heads and whispered amongst each other. "What's the matter?"

Ayzili knelt down next to Carlos. "The deep waters are home to many creatures even the baka fear."

"Creatures?" the poison harvester said. He slammed his box down on the sand with more force than he should have. "They're lwa, newly dead. We shouldn't stir up Agwe."

Carlos realized what he was suggesting, that they literally set sail across the underworld, home to the spirits of the dead. It explained the reaction he was getting. But the current drifted in their favor. He could see it out beyond the waves, flowing steadily back to the city. They would return to Ginen much faster that way and could carry twice the poison.

"Let's start the raft," Ayzili said, rising with an air of finality in her voice. No one questioned her. They knew she was right.

A cluster of driftwood poles broke the crest of a far dune. Carlos and Ayzili made for them, leaving behind three of the men to harvest as much of the blowfish poison as they could.

With a few blows of an axe, the timbers fell to the ground, making Carlos wonder if they were too brittle to withstand the surf. At least it would be easy carrying them back to the shore. They made several trips and in no time had assembled a healthy collection of logs. Carlos pinched a splinter from his palm and squinted beyond the dunes. The sun remained high, but he doubted they could finish the raft before it set. Ayzili seemed to read his mind.

"We'll leave at first light," she said.

"Of course we will." One of the men looked over at them. "Even priests don't travel the night water."

"The priests sail?" Carlos asked.

"Yes," she paused, caught up in a thought.

"And how do they avoid the sea creatures?"

"They only sail once a year. During the festival of Agwe, the priests take a small raft and load it with offerings: champagne, carvings, and silks. They tow it out to sea, over Agwe's home, then let it sink."

"It's for Lasiren too," the teen said, the fear gone from his face.

"Agwe's wife." Ayzili pointed to her slender calves. "No legs, like a fish."

"Mermaid?

Ayzili nodded and then kicked one of the logs into position. "Let's hope Agwe doesn't mistake us for an offering." She winked at Carlos. None of the other men laughed, however. Off in the distance, they could see storm clouds gathering.

Chapter 24

The archive's collections seemed to be divided by age - not a very efficient system, especially if you were searching by topic. The older texts were all written in Latin or Greek, the newer ones English or Spanish. If only we could find some sort of card catalogue, Henry thought. He stretched out his back muscles, which had long since developed a severe crick.

"Anything interesting?" he called over the racks.

Jell's voice came echoing across, "Everything's interesting..."

Henry smiled. This was true. Already they'd uncovered texts on death rites, marriage, and creation myths. It would take a lifetime to fully absorb the information contained in this cavern. But they didn't have that kind of time. They needed to find the baka's Achilles' heel. And they needed to find it fast.

Henry sat on one of the benches that dotted the archives. He'd worked up a sweat rifling through the parchments. His throat felt dry, and he wondered if Jell had anything to drink. Before he yelled out, however, he stopped and listened. He heard the gurgle of water, distant but unmistakable.

Following the sound, he traversed deep into the parchment forest. The rows opened up into a small clearing, where Henry discovered the source of the noise: a fountain. Looking carefully at it, he realized this could be the key to everything.

* * *

The two groups set to work without much talk. Ayzili, Carlos, and the teenager tied together their logs with leather straps, while the harvesters moved from fish to fish, gathering the poison. A pile of the wax boxes slowly grew at their side.

"We've never collected this much yamala," one of the men remarked. They were mashing several of the lungs into each box to save space. Sweat stained the harvester's brow, and his hands shook from the concentration.

"Careful," said his friend. "Don't rush."

A hundred yards back towards the ocean, Carlos pulled taut a final leather strap. He stood back to admire their work. The raft appeared seaworthy – provided they had calm seas. It could easily accommodate the ten survivors and their cargo. The stern even had a tent to provide some relief from the sun.

"What should we call her?" Carlos asked.

"Imamou," Ayzili said under her breath.

Carlos looked at her quizzically. "What's that?"

"We should call it a raft," Ayzili said, turning serious, "and we should finish loading the yamala tonight."

"There's a lot left," the teen groaned. "Let's wait for morning."

Carlos shook his head. "Too risky."

"That's risky? And sailing into —" the teen began, but Ayzili cast him a look, and he slumped off to gather more wax boxes. His feet dragged through the tide pools, now reflecting the deep crimson of an evening sky. A fiery sunset blazed into existence, then fell victim to a bank of storm clouds that moved in and extinguished it. A stiff breeze rippled across the water, signaling the arrival of a front. Carlos noticed another movement in one of the pools. No, that was a reflection. What he was seeing stood on the dune beyond. Something had crested its ridge – a large shape. He bolted upright.

"Oh shit. They've returned."

More shapes started to appear on the horizon, hundreds of them, their legs skittering over the crest. This was not another baka scouting party - it was an army. By her reaction, he could tell Ayzili saw them too. The men harvesting the poison, however, had their backs to the desert and kept working, unaware.

"Hey," Ayzili screamed at the top of her lungs and waved wildly. But the men were too far out of earshot. Carlos grabbed a blanket from the raft and sprinted off in their direction. As he passed the teen he yelled over his shoulder, "We're leaving now. There's too many to fight."

The baka were already descending the dunes, pouring across the ridge and onto the flatland. Fortunately, it was low tide so this stretch extended quite far. It would buy them a few precious seconds. By now, the men had felt the earth tremors, seen the baka, and were desperately grabbing as many poison boxes as they could carry.

"Stop. Lay them here." Carlos unfurled the blanket and began laying boxes on top of it. After they'd transferred the pile, he started to drag it towards the raft. The other men joined him in the effort but it was slow going, the wet sand providing too much friction.

"We're not going to make it," one of them said, thunderstruck at the advancing wall of baka.

"Go help Ayzili push the raft out," Carlos yelled. "Go. Now!" As he said it, he tripped on one of the deeper pools and splashed into the sand. It burned like sandpaper across his forearms. Another of the men helped him to his feet.

"We have to go faster," Carlos said. He grit his teeth and dug into the wet sand, dragging the makeshift sled ever forward. The first wave of baka loomed close enough that he could make out their eyes. The creatures were charging forward with all their might, a stampeding mass of claws and legs.

"We need to loose some of the boxes," he said. "Drop a third of them."

The men protested. "That's a year's worth —"

"It's that or nothing." A stern look told them exactly what nothing meant. The men quickly ditched the top layer of boxes, and they picked up speed. But the baka kept pace, still flooding down the dunes by the hundreds. The creatures had formed a gigantic semicircle around them, tightening the noose step by step. Their only escape was the sea.

There must be thousands of them, Carlos thought, hundreds of thousands. He had trouble thinking over the drowning cacophony of scraping shells. With a great splash, the first rows of baka hit the tidal pools. The spray they churned up reflected gold in the evening sun. Looking back to the sea, Carlos saw that Ayzili and the other men had succeeded in moving the raft out into the surf and were holding it steady amidst the waves. But they were still a hundred yards away.

He stared into the eyes of the other men; there was no need for words. They all knew what they had to do. Ignoring the pain, they dug in with their heels and pulled with all their remaining strength. The makeshift sled rocketed across the sand and, after what seemed an eternity, Carlos felt the rush of seawater across his ankles.

"I'll hold off the first few," Ayzili yelled. "Start loading the raft." She had already withdrawn her bow and was aiming down the length of an arrow. Picking a target, she let fly. A baka, who'd foolishly split from the pack, caught her arrow mid-stride. It tripped and spiraled into the tide pools, spraying forth a saltwater fan.

Carlos tried to tune out the noise. He concentrated on tossing the poison bricks to the teen, who stacked them as quickly as he could. There was no time to be gentle. Out of the corner of his eye, Carlos could see baka falling to their deaths all around them. Their screams came louder and more often now, every few seconds.

He snuck a look at Ayzili. Her biceps strained from bending the bow back so rapidly. Lines of sweat rolled down her forehead. But what gave him the most pause was the look in her eye as she turned towards him – a steady gaze void of fear. The arrow launched from her bow and whizzed past his cheek. He heard the baka's scream, felt water on the back of his neck, but ignored it all and tossed the last poison brick. The teen caught it and slapped it down on top of the others. It was time to go.

"Tie them down," Carlos yelled as he cast the wet blanket up and over the boxes like a fishing net. Then he leaned against the wood and pushed hard. The raft jostled through the remains of a wave, and he tasted saltwater as it gurgled in around him. Focus, he told himself. If they headed into the breakers now, without securing the boxes, they would loose their poisonous cargo. The whole expedition would be in vain.

"Hurry. Throw me a strap." He doubled it around a log and tied a quick knot. As he cinched it tight, he felt a sharp pain slice through his shirt and tear across his back.

"Carlos," Ayzili screamed and pulled him onto the raft. With her free hand she hacked at a claw with her sword.

Hell had erupted around them. The baka were swarming, and it was only the water level that kept them from overwhelming the raft. The tidal pools teemed with movement and every last survivor now engaged in close combat. Over the tarp, Carlos could see some of the baka circling past the raft. Soon they would be totally surrounded.

"Cover me," he yelled, not sure if they'd understand what he meant. Slipping past the belly of one of the creatures, Carlos held his breath and kicked beneath the raft. The saltwater stung his cuts, but he ignored the pain. He could see the frenzied movement of baka legs thrashing about as he pulled himself towards the front.

Surfacing, he grabbed one of the straps and leaned into the water. The momentum was slow, but he could feel the raft pulling forward. The waves fought his every step, almost knocking him down a few times. He stood his ground, however, and pushed forward. The raft jolted now from baka attempt to board it. They were so numerous, even Ayzili could no longer fend them off. Out of the corner of his eye, he spotted several large ones wading towards him. In a few seconds they'd be within striking range. He closed his eyes and dug his feet into the soft sand.

When he opened them he saw the dripping silhouette of a monstrous baka, only yards away. At the same moment, Carlos felt his shirt cling wet against his skin. The water was receding. And he knew why. Beyond the baka loomed a wave, a tall one.

"Hold on," he yelled and laid himself flat against the poison boxes. As the baka moved in to strike, the raft connected with a wall of water. The creature let out a startled cry, but its noise was instantly muffled.

Carlos found himself fully submerged in the crushing surf. Through blurred vision, he saw a current of bubbles sweep the crab away.

Then sunlight and noise returned; the raft burst out from the rolling wave and came crashing back down. They were through the breakers. A mass of scrambling baka lay in their wake, and nothing but the open ocean lay ahead. They were free.

Chapter 25

The fountain took Henry's breath away. About the size of a carousel, it had carvings of baka decorating its edge. They surrounded a low pool, from which a short pillar rose. A jet of water gurgled atop this column, sparkling in the torchlight and sending reflections across the cavern walls. This light show also bathed a sword in the center of the spray. The weapon plunged downward through the water stream, like the Arthurian myth, except this blade was thinner and more ornate.

"I've never seen a sword like that," Jell said.

"A rapier, Spanish by the look of it," Henry encircled the weapon. A series of complex, sweeping rings festooned its hilt. "Probably belonged to a Conquistador." As he rounded the fountain, Henry noticed the pool itself wasn't a perfect circle.

"It's heart shaped," he said, scratching his beard. The base had two bulges that formed the unmistakable shape. So the fountain's a heart pierced by a sword, Henry thought, but instead of blood it pumps water.

"That's the veve for Ayzili," Jell said, "a fierce protector lwa."

"Hmmm, explains the sword." Somehow, Henry wasn't surprised. It made sense to pay homage to a fierce spirit if you wanted to protect the archives. But his gut told him there was more here.

"We need to keep looking through the scrolls," Jell said, turning away.

"No, Riyal would've already done that." Henry sat down at the edge of the fountain. "I think the answers we seek are encoded here."

"But there's no text."

"In the Middle Ages..." Henry began but saw that Jell didn't understand. "In my world, there was a time when lessons were told in stone, through statues and wall reliefs. Maybe the people who built this place were trying to do the same thing – teach us something regardless what language we speak."

"Who do you think carved this fountain?" Jell asked.

Henry twisted his university ring, lost in thought. "The Taino Indians, Conquistadors, lost British colonists...maybe all of the above," he said with a hint of excitement in his voice.

* * *

The current pulled their raft away from the shore, but no one minded at this point. As each swell reached its peak, the expedition party was given fresh views of the baka army, retreating angrily from the surf. The creatures now covered the dunes like ants, rows of them stretching off into the distance.

"They've formed ranks," Carlos said in awe, "like a human army."

Ayzili frowned. "They've brought water. That's a bad sign."

A few of the crabs bunched around what appeared to be giant sea anemones, tugging at their tentacles like a litter of nursing puppies.

"They only bring water on extended sieges," Ayzili explained. Then she fell silent, starring at the ridge of a far dune. Framed amongst the hulking shadows of the baka, stood the silhouette of a solitary man. The figure stared at them for some time and then turned and walked down the opposite slope.

"Traitor." Ayzili sunk her sword into the raft and collapsed next to it. "I hope they eat him alive." Carlos noticed that the man next to her was bleeding severely across the chest.

"Where are you cut?" he asked him.

"Everywhere."

Carlos tore a piece of the blanket off the box tarp. "Apply pressure to the wound." The man grimaced and did so. The cloth instantly turned crimson and then started to run as water mixed with the blood. Raindrops were falling from the sky, just a few at first, and then the clouds let loose with a strong downpour. Most of the men huddled up under the tarp. But Ayzili stood at the bow of the raft, staring blankly into the water ahead. As the deluge increased, the water's surface broke with thousands of miniature explosions.

"What are you looking at?" Carlos asked, joining her. She parted a strand of wet hair from her eyes.

"Out here's where I left my husband." This was the last thing he'd expected her to say. He studied her face to gauge the emotion, but there was none to read. Either that, or she was skilled at masking it.

Rain streamed down her hair, highlighting the angular features of her cheekbones.

"He was buried at sea?" Carlos asked. She nodded. "How did he die?"

"The same way you and I will, crushed beneath a baka's claw." Ayzili winced as she pulled the memories from her subconscious. Then her jaw tightened. "My husband was a high priest. Years ago he joined an expedition like this, to say the harvest prayers." Her eyes stared off into the distance.

"The baka attacked his party. He was wounded." She swallowed. "After he died, I sailed out here to release the body. I left my son at home, alone and unprotected." Her face said the rest, and Carlos had enough tact not to inquire further.

"Don't blame yourself," he said, staring into the water, black as ink. For a moment, he thought he saw a flicker of movement deep below - probably one of those huge blowfish, he figured

"The baka that killed my son was small. If I'd been there..." Ayzili broke off. "You still believe you can fight them all?"

"We've got enough poison here to kill a million, at least. If we arm every man in Ginen —"

"We lost fourteen, Carlos," she sighed. "Fourteen fighting one baka legion. One." She stressed the number by holding up a finger. "Hundreds of legions live in the dune sea. And there aren't enough hands or weapons to kill them all." The teen eyed them nervously from across the raft, so Ayzili lowered her voice. "These are the death throes of our people. If you want to survive, you'd best leave while you still can."

"I lost someone too, once. I wasn't there to protect her." He didn't need to complete the thought – his message was clear. He wasn't running away.

Ayzili turned her gaze from the horizon to stare at him. "I don't need protecting."

"I can see that."

Her long fingers pushed back the hair from her face again. The storm had lightened up now, and a thin mist left drops on her eyelashes. "You lost a child?"

Carlos nodded. "Almost a year ago. She was sick." He swallowed hard. "You need to move on." Even as the words escaped his lips, they seemed hollow. He was a hypocrite, giving advice he'd never followed himself.

"I didn't kill the baka. So my son..." Ayzili faltered. Saying this was taking a toll of her, but she continued anyway. "Unless it died, which it likely didn't, his soul's trapped in that shell."

"Inside the baka?"

She shook her head, yes.

"You want justice?" But as he said it, he realized it was much more than that. She really felt that the soul of her son was trapped inside the shell of a monster - physically trapped there. Is this the fate of all devoured by the baka? He now understood why she looked so pained.

"You know the path of the dead?" she said, staring into the water. "The souls swim in the low waters for over a year and a day." She watched the swells rise and fall. "Then there's a ceremony, a beautiful one, when we reclaim them from the depths. They enter the govi jars and rest forever. Their spirit's finally at peace. And they won't torment us anymore." A tear ran down her cheek. "We should sleep," Ayzili said, trying to soothe the knot that had marred her brow.

"You've not performed this ceremony for your husband or son?" Carlos asked.

"One day, I will." Ayzili smiled and curled up near the edge of the raft. She folded her arms behind her head and closed her eyes. "One day soon."

"Yeah, we should turn in."

Carlos gazed across the raft at Ayzili. A chasm of experience separated him from this woman. She couldn't be more different. Why then, he asked himself, do I feel so close to her?

A full moon lit up the raft and reflected disjointedly in the ocean below. All was silent now save the gentle lapping of water against timbers. Occasionally, fabric rustled as one of the expedition members shifted in their sleep. Carlos couldn't join them, however. Too many thoughts drifted through his mind at the moment, chief among them, Ayzili's contradictions.

So often she seemed to abandon hope, her words laced with morbid humor - while at other times, she was all that kept them going. She'd shown great contempt for anything sacred - yet when she spoke of this ceremony to honor the dead, he'd seen her smile. A battle certainly raged inside her as fierce as the one she fought with her sword. Which side will win? He wasn't sure. But he was pretty certain death was the cause of all that turmoil. That much he knew from experience.

Carlos watched a layer of clouds engulf the moon, plunging the raft into shadow. Then he heard a splash. It was not loud enough to cause alarm, likely just a fish, but still he sat upright.

In the darkness, he saw the silhouette of Ayzili crouched at one end of the raft. She lay on her belly, legs dangling over the side like a swimmer pushing out from the pool. Long strings of hair fell across her face and gleamed wet. Had she been swimming? The cloud passed from the moon and instantly, the raft was bathed in light.

It was not Ayzili crouching there, for she still lay curled up at the far edge of the raft. Looming over her was what appeared to be a drowned woman, beautiful and eerily still. Her skin glistened pale and green in the moonlight, the color of kelp. Dark, dripping hair fell over two of the largest eyes Carlos had ever seen. And they locked on him.

Before Carlos could make a sound, the stranger threw herself onto Ayzili, rolling them both into the water with surprising agility. Ayzili gave a yell, but it was cut short as the two disappeared beneath the dark surface with the flip of a silvery tail.

"Hey!" Carlos jumped to his feet, his shout stirring the others.

"What happened?" the men asked.

"Something grabbed Ayzili." Carlos ran to the edge of the raft and peered down. He could see shapes moving deep in the water, indistinct and blurry. Without thinking, he took a deep breath and pushed off from the wood. As he connected with the waterline, a freezing jolt shocked him from the fog of sleep.

The shouts of the expedition members fell to silence in this eerie world. Below he could see two dark shapes struggling deeper into the depths. One was pulling the other steadily downward. They were heading into what should have been darkness. But instead, they swam into a river of light. It reminded Carlos of a night drive through Miami, headlights winding along the Palmetto Expressway. Thousands of individual globs pulsed in rhythm like a great vein – jellyfish. With strong kicks. Carlos pressed into this highway of light.

He couldn't make out the details of the jellies, but he felt their sting. Lines of fire flashed across his arm as the unseen tentacles grazed his skin. The forms of Ayzili and her captor were rapidly vanishing amidst the swarms of glowing creatures. Their numbers were so thick now that the water below teemed with them, almost seemed to boil. It was like staring into the sun. Through this glare, he caught Ayzili's head staring back at him with one last, imploring look, but she was soon yanked away into the tangle of stinging light. The pain overwhelmed Carlos. He relented, cried out, and felt his body drift back to the surface. Barely conscious, the last thing he remembered were the hands of the other men dragging him aboard the raft.

* * *

"Let's take this piece by piece. What do we have?" Henry stared at the fountain, hoping the answers might strike him in a flash of insight.

"The only carvings I recognize are those veves," Jell said, pointing to the stepping-stones scattered across the water like lily pads. Strange carved symbols decorated each stump. "Five symbols, five spirits...," Jell said thoughtfully. Henry squinted at one that looked like an ornate cross.

He wasn't sure what to make of the lwa symbols, so he turned to the other carvings. Those are baka, right?" He gestured to the bass relief along the inside wall of the pool. The carvings depicted a ring of crabs just above the waterline.

Jell knelt down to inspect the nearest one. Although half-submerged in the water, he could still make out its pincers. "Yes, I've seen a baka do this before with its claws. They sweep the water into their mouths. That's how they drink."

"Where did you see a baka drinking water?"

"It wasn't water," Jell said grimly and left it at that.

Henry swallowed hard. His throat was dry and parched, however, so he motioned to the fountain. "Safe to drink?"

"Yes. It's likely the same as flows from the falls above."

Cupping his hands, Henry took a long sip. The water tasted cool and sweet with a hint of copper. He examined the sword rising from the fountain's center, its hilt sparkling with pearl-sized droplets. Up close, the blade looked razor sharp. It had taken a great deal of skill to forge such a weapon and even more to etch the designs into its metal. Suddenly, Henry's eyes lit up.

"What is it?" Jell asked.

He grinned. "I think I know how to kill the baka," he said, "every last one of them."

CPSIA information can be obtained
at www.ICGtesting.com
Printed in the USA
LVHW081342221222
735718LV00014B/554

9 781837 615070